IN

HOT

WATER

[a Tijuana love story]

Tucker A. Pickett

In Hot Water, a Tijuana Love Story

a novel

Copyright © 2012 Tucker A. Pickett

Cover Design by Bradley Pickett

For bookings, interviews, or any other author information please contact Tucker Pickett at tuckerpickett@hotmail.com or the Facebook™ page *In Hot Water*

First Printing by CV Graphics and Design

Printed in the United States of America

ISBN 0-615-71572-8

"Being a woman is a terribly difficult task, since it consists principally in dealing with men."

— Joseph Conrad

In Hot Water…

Part I

I

Gaby Romero was born in the United States. She lives in Mexico. Gaby works and goes to school in the United States. She crosses the border every day. Sometimes, twice a day. On the rare occasion, three times day. She once told me, "I don't feel like I've done anything unless I cross the border." I asked her, "Which way?" Her reply: "Either way." Half of her family lives in the United States. The other half lives in Mexico. When they all get together, and they often do, the family has to decide on which side. They take turns. On a map, two different cities exist. One, called San Diego, sits on the northern side of the border. The other, Tijuana, exists on the southern side. According to Gaby it is one big city, and the border is just a man-made nuisance. The border is a reality to the people that live here and make their living here, but it is a reality they would rather do without. Gaby has developed an intuition concerning the border; when to cross, when not to cross, which lanes move quickly, which lanes crawl to the border for hours on end. When I need advice on how to cross the border, I just ask her. The Tijuana border crossing is its own special world, and the people that have to deal with it every day learn the ebb and flow of border.

When you get down to it, the city of Tijuana is one of the most beautiful in the world. Not beautiful in the physical sense; Tijuana can be about as ugly as they come. But beautiful in a spiritual sense. Tijuana is a beautiful city if you have the right eye. When I first met Gaby I asked her if Tijuana was dangerous. She replied "Sure, it's dangerous. Everyplace is dangerous if you're looking for it."

I once asked Gaby where she is from. She replied, "Mexico." I asked her how she knew that, because she was born in the States. She answered "Because I'm Mexican." I found that strange. I asked her again, "Weren't you born in the United States? Don't you go to school in the United States? Isn't your family living in the United States?" She responded "yes" to everything. So, I finished off, "Are you still Mexican?" She replied without hesitation and with a smile on her lips, "yes." I asked, "How do you know?" She just gave me a shrug.

Gaby is a complicated woman.

To be honest though, she is just as complicated as the city of Tijuana. Gaby is not the only border resident with an identity crisis. Patriotism always runs deep in border towns, and Tijuana is no exception. Attitudes are magnified because the conflict is artificial. Gaby identifies herself as Mexican, and she is not the only border commuter. The actual number is in the thousands. Many are going to work. Some are going to school. A few are going to shop.

Some are crossing for the first time. A couple are crossing for the last time. Some are crossing something for the first time. In the world of Tijuana, just about anything goes and just about everybody crosses at one time or another. Gaby has told me that she loves Tijuana and she hates Tijuana, and if that sounds equivocal she apologizes. Tijuana is unusual in that it brings out the best and worst in people. It certainly brings out the best in her, and maybe the worst in me.

I don't know why whenever I find myself alone in Tijuana I start thinking of Gaby, but I always do. I always go back to that place in my brain where she resides, and it is always brought out by the strange vibrations this town puts out. Gaby is as convoluted as this city is. That connection is there for me. However, that is a compliment. Everybody needs a little disorder in their lives. It keeps you on your toes. Stagnation is something to be avoided. The realities of Tijuana don't allow it. Gaby represents it.

II

"Evan, why do I always have to pick you up? You're supposed to be the man."

"What? I am the guy, but since you drive a Mercedes and all, I figured you would want to show off all over the road."

In Europe, Mercedes are cab cars, but here I feel more important when I'm in an eighty-thousand dollar vehicle. However, Gaby doesn't seem interested in chauffeuring me around.

"Well, you figured wrong. You're driving this time. I'm not driving down there with all those drunks on the road. Let's take your car. I'll drive then."

"No, no. I'll drive. It's impossible for me to ride shotgun with you driving anyways."

There is no traffic as we cross the border into Tijuana. I enjoy riding as a passenger in a classic Mercedes Benz, but I don't enjoy driving one down the streets of Tijuana. There is pressure in getting behind the wheel of a vehicle of this caliber. It attracts too much attention. The wrong kind of attention. Both of our windows are rolled down to let the air in. It was hot today, but cooled down as soon as the sun disappeared. I prefer the fresh air tonight. The traffic is light in the city right now. The heavy traffic is always coming out of Tijuana. Mexico has a very efficient model of allowing vehicles past customs. You drive through a lane, wait for a light—red or green; every tenth car gets red—and drive on by. Very efficient, and contributes to almost no line going into Tijuana. We pass, get our green light, and enter the spontaneous and disorderly city of Tijuana. Spontaneous because anything can happen down here, and disorderly because nobody seems to care what happens down here. We drive over the bridge and into the *Zona Rio* of Tijuana. This is where much of the legitimate action occurs in the city. The Avenues of the River Zone are intersected with flowing gloriettas; a circular traffic pattern with a statue of somebody in the center. These gloriettas are difficult to navigate; you must merge into the flowing traffic and exit just as smoothly. Cutting people off is perfectly acceptable and expected. The only sin of the glorietta is to disrupt the flow of traffic.

As I approach the first glorietta I ignore the stop sign and try to merge in. A large bus cuts me off so I swerve around him and make my way into the middle lane. As I drive around and through the back-side of the glorietta I cut off another car that was trying to get around me. Gloriettas are always a circus during high traffic time. The best way to approach them is move with the flow. Never stop. The same holds for Tijuana. The only sin of the city is to interrupt the flow of the city. Tijuana has a unique vibe: spontaneous, disorderly, and perverse. If you accept this, you'll do fine. If you fight it, you will hate this city. Many do. Most Americans do. Americans demand certain ideals from their cities, orderliness being at the top of the list. Tijuana is the antithesis of most American cities. It is the Yin to San Diego's Yang. If you embrace spontaneity, then you will embrace this city. If you are perverse, this will be your hometown. It begins with driving; driving to the local bars and clubs.

"Alright, so where we going?"

"I was thinking Plaza del Zapato," Gaby says. "I feel like a few beers first. We can try Sótano Suizo." Gaby always wants to go to Suizo. She loves that bar.

"What? La Plaza is dying out," I reply. "Hardly anybody goes there anymore."

"I'm somebody, and I like going there. I remember when it opened."

"You don't remember that. You must have been sixteen at the time."

"Exactly."

I'm bothered by this. It's never fair. Women have all of the advantages.

"In this city, if you're a woman with a pretty face and a decent body, you don't need an identification card. You just need to be willing to take advantage of your attributes," I tell her.

"That's insulting. I just use what I have, like anybody else would do. You're just a hypocrite, that's all. If you had the chance to enter clubs under-age, you would have, and you know it."

"Your appearance is your meal ticket," I say. "It's unfair. I had to bide my time."

"What, you want me to feel sorry for you? Here I go, feeling sorry for you because you couldn't get into bars when you were a kid."

I look over, and I laugh. Alright, then. "Plaza?"

"La Plaza it is."

"Suizo sounds good to me."

As we arrive I pay the cover, of course. Gaby would never in a million years pay the cover. If I asked her because I was broke, she would of course say "Yes" and pay the cover. She would not even let on that she was upset by it, but deep down it would ruin her night. See, Gaby wants the best of both worlds. I believe it to be unfair. Why do I pay every time? The man always pays, pays for everything. If you want something in life, you have to pay for it. You have to pay for everything you want out of life. No questions asked; no complaints filed. I should not have to pay the cover everywhere we go. I wonder who made up that rule. Chivalry, I guess. Those punks ruined it for all of us, one thousand years ago. I am mulling this over as we make our way into the bar.

Sótano Suizo is right across the border, where the locals hang out. You won't find many Americans or tourists in here. Nice, long bar, with a few curves in it. If a bar has curves in it, like a good woman, you know it is expensive. The wood is rich, and well polished. I appreciate a good, polished, curving, well maintained bar. A lot of money put into it. Right in the middle of "Plaza del Zapato," named after the shoe bazaar right next to it. During the day, this place is a shoe bazaar. At night, the bars, clubs, taco stands and hot-dog stands open up. Plaza del Zapato is what they call it. The Shoe Plaza. Also, the social scene in Tijuana. Or it used to be, anyway. The scene always changes in Tijuana. A place gets big, then it gets crowded. Then the drugs arrive, and it fucks everything up. The drugs arrived in Plaza Zapato a few years ago. There is a bar called 'Pancho Villa'. Most people in there are high. I never go in there. It's dangerous, especially if you are just out to enjoy yourself and have a good time. It's violent in there half of the time. Once the violence starts, time to pack up and move on. Sótano Suizo isn't that way...yet.

The bartender recognizes Gaby and greets her with a kiss on the cheek. He barely looks at me. I have to get his attention to order.

"Clamato for her, Bohemia for me." I always order Bohemia, a great beer. Bohemia is beer for any occasion, and it goes down well. Gaby's clamato is like a Bloody Mary, but substitute beer for vodka.

"Wait. I don't want to drink clamato. I want a drink."

"I know, I know. Relax, it is a drink. Trust me."

What's in it?"

"Clamato, beer, lime, and some other stuff."

The secret ingredients to a good clamato, or clamacheve, are strange, and don't make sense, but for some reason they come out right.

"What 'other' stuff?"

"Don't worry about it. Try it first and then I'll tell you what they put in it."

"I don't want anything weird."

"Don't worry; they're not putting anything illegal in it, or anything else unusual in your drink. Just give it a shot."

The bartender finally arrives with our drinks. My glass is frosty cold. In Sótano Suizo they frost your glass before they pour the beer into it. All bars and restaurants should do this. Every beer should be served in a frosty mug. Gaby's clama-cheve is red-orange, bubbling, with chamoy on the rim of the glass. She takes a sip.

"This is bizarre."

"But good."

"Yeah, it's pretty good."

"No, it's better than 'pretty good.' Admit it."

"It's alright."

I know she enjoys it. She just doesn't want to admit that I am right, or actually know something. If she didn't want it, she would pretend to be disgusted and make me drink it. The fact that she is still drinking it is evidence that she enjoys the "clama-cheve." I give her the history of the beer.

"Tijuana is the only place in the world that you will find the clama-cheve."

"No, it's not. Like you said, it's like a Bloody-Mary, but with beer. It's a poor man's Bloody-Mary."

"No, it's more than that. You remember that secret ingredient? Well, it's Worcestershire sauce. I swear, Worcestershire sauce, and it works. I've made a few myself, and it gives it that extra snap. One-quarter Clamato, three-quarters beer, with a splash of lime juice, Worcestershire sauce, hot sauce, salt, and there you go."

"I don't believe you. How do they even know about Worcestershire sauce in a place like T.J.? And who would think about putting it in a drink like this?"

"In T.J., they'll try anything."

15

"That, I'll believe."

We sit at the bar and talk. We have a nice conversation. School is going well for her. She thinks she is going to get her best grades yet. Gaby can't wait to graduate. I tell her things are picking up at the bar. Maybe I can make bartender soon. She gives me an odd look at that. "You should think about something long term," she tells me. "Bartending" is not a productive career, I'm told. I should find something better, or go back to school. I ask Gaby what school has done for her, and she replies, "Wait and see." The conversation is friendly, and lively. Her bartender friend steps into our conversation and says you can make a great living tending a bar. I agree with him. I'm not angry with him anymore. Gaby complains that we are ganging up on her. We reply that any trade is a good trade if you are dedicated to your skill and willing to work hard. Bartending takes a certain skill, like anything else, and some people are better at it than others. She agrees.

I am on my third beer and starting to warm up. I drink Bohemia while I'm in Tijuana, and it is one of the best beers, period. I consider myself quite the beer connoisseur, and Bohemia is at the top of the list. As a friend once told me, "This is a man's beer." It is. Unlike the typical 4.8 alcohol content found in most lagers, Bohemia carries a 5.3, yet is smooth like a good lager should be. No aftertaste. In beer, when alcohol content goes up, the taste alters. It all comes down to how the beer is brewed, what type of hops you use, and how long the beer is allowed to ferment. The longer a beer ferments, the higher the alcohol content is. Consequently, the bitterness factor increases as well. A good brewer knows how to master his ingredients. Bohemia is strong, yet tastes light. It is a well crafted beer. You can drink a Bohemia at eight in the morning just as easily as you can at eight in the evening. I can wake up and have a Bohemia.

Gaby sips her drink, then scans the bar. She's always occupied with something else. She can never pay attention to what's in front of her. She finds what she is looking for. "Hey, I'm going over there to say hello to a few friends. Keep my seat warm."

"Alright."

Gaby always does this. It occurs almost every time we are down here. Gaby knows everybody down here, and we always bump into an old friend. At a bar, club, mall, grocery store, at a traffic light, bank, taco stand, abarrotes, wherever, there is always an old friend or two. Half the time she doesn't even bother to introduce me. She just excuses herself to go say 'hi'. The problem is 'hello' consumes half an hour. I look over to the other table and notice that the 'old friends' are a couple of other guys. Fine with me; this bar is packed. Plenty of people to get to know. There are good looking women everywhere, most without escorts. Two can play at that game. There's plenty of 'old friends' in here for me as well. I'll show her. I look up at the T.V. on top of the bar and watch some soccer game playing half way around the world. Some European club playing another European club.

I finish the whole second half by myself.

III

I'm about to walk out of Sótano Suizo when Gaby decides to stroll back on over.

"Evan, I'm sorry. But I haven't seen Oscar in years. He's a cousin of mine."

"A cousin? Why didn't you tell me? Why not invite me over?"

"What, you wanted to come over? You looked like you were enjoying the game. Well, he's more like a second cousin. He's actually from Obregon. I haven't seen him in years. I was surprised to see him here. Did you want to come over? He's still over there."

"No, don't worry about it now."

"Sorry, but he's family."

Like that makes it better. And he's no cousin. He's probably a second cousin, thrice removed. I don't consider that family. Neither would the Catholic Church. They could legally marry. I don't buy that 'family' routine. Gaby catches my eye, and tries to smooth things over.

"Sorry, but I know stuff like that doesn't bother you," she tells me. "Let's have a drink; together this time."

I order two more. No more beer for me. Straight scotch, please.

"Don't get into the heavy stuff," she tells me.

"What? What the hell. Don't ignore me for an hour, then tell me what to do. If I want a scotch on the rocks, I'll have a scotch on the rocks."

"I'm not telling you what to do, and it wasn't an hour."

"I finished the whole second half of a soccer game."

"You did?"

Whatever. I didn't want to chat up her second cousin anyway. I change the subject. I want to avoid an argument.

"So, how's Sonia?"

"My cousin? Sonia Tellez?"

"Yes, your cousin. What other 'Sonia's' do we know?"

"Well, I know a few. Anyway, she's fine. Still with Adrian. I just had lunch with them yesterday."

"Oh, really," I say. "Still with Adrian, huh?"

"Don't say it like that. Give him a chance. Oh, also, he's looking for work. Do you know anything? Sonia wanted me to ask you."

"I can ask, but I don't think so. He did ask me that a while back. I'll look around for something. Maybe another bar."

Actually, I do have something Adrian can help me with. I can't mention it to Gaby, however. I have certain reservations about involving Adrian. He's too close to my social circle. There are certain activities Gaby doesn't need to know about.

"Help him out if you can," Gaby asks me. "Sonia would appreciate it."

"I'll see what I can do. How are the rest of your cousins? Where's Eduardo? I miss that guy."

"We all miss him, but he's up in school right now. He needs to focus, so don't bother him with stuff down here. Everybody else is fine."

"You're crazy. Living in a dorm in college is worse than here. Isn't he living in a fraternity house?"

"Yes, but he's renting a room. He's not actually part of the frat."

"How does that work? Does he get to enjoy all of the benefits?"

"I don't know. I don't think he pledged. Ask him when he comes back down. Anyway, we should see Eduardo later on this week. He's always down here on weekends."

"Yeah, that guy loves Tijuana more than I do."

"You don't love Tijuana."

"Yes I do, I just don't appreciate being ignored for two hours."

"It wasn't two hours."

"Yes it was. It was the second half of a soccer match."

"Ok, I'll make it up to you, if you're going to insist on being upset. What do you want to do? I'll go wherever."

I have plenty of places in mind, and they require the whole night. Maybe I can use this to my advantage.

"Let's get out of here. We can go up to Agua Caliente. Let's find a restaurant."

"Alright, that sounds fine."

I knew that would straighten her out. Gaby is always game for a meal in the Zona Rio. As we stand up and straighten ourselves up to leave, Gaby's cousin walks over to us.

"Won't you guys stay? I've got next round. By the way, I'm Oscar."

"Evan Blake," I reply.

Gaby turns to him, "Oscar, thanks. But we have a date up in Agua Caliente."

"Fine dining?"

"Something like that," I say.

"Well, enjoy yourselves."

"Don't worry, we will." I smile at him as I say it. He gives me a strange look, then returns to his table.

"You don't need to be rude," Gaby explains to me.

"I wasn't rude. I was just giving him the facts."

"Your name is a tough name down here. I don't know how you spend so much time in Tijuana with a name like 'Evan Blake.' "

"It works. I've never seen you complain about my name before."

"I was just thinking—you know, 'Gabriela Blake.' It doesn't ring well in the ear."

"You can keep your last name."

"I wasn't planning on changing it."

Gaby and I walk out hand in hand.

We drive over to Casa Plasencia and find parking right in front. I ask Gaby if she wants to sit at a table or at the bar. She replies that she doesn't mind. Casa Plasencia is a nice two-story restaurant, with a bar on the second floor.

The bar has a side entrance with stairs leading up to it. Gaby has her arm locked under mine. Gaby can do this; switch gears as quick as anybody. There is a phrase in Argentina: *Perro Amor.* The literal translation is "Dog Love," but the actual translation is something much more sinister. As close as I can get to English is "Love-Hate," but with heavier connotations. That's as close as I can describe my current relationship with Gaby; "Perro Amor." One minute I'm ready to walk out of a bar on her account, and the next we're walking hand in hand and enjoying each other's company. I can't figure it out. That's the way it is with her. Gaby has her whole life planned out twenty years in advance, but she is totally clueless to things right in front of her.

There is a small line to get into the bar, but Gaby never waits in a line. We walk right up to the door, the attendant takes one look at Gaby, spares a glance for me, then lets us in without a hassle. I hear a few people complain, but that's their problem. We sit down at the last two available seats at the bar. There are fringe benefits to dating somebody like Gaby. Waiting in line to get into a bar or club is beneath her. It's her attitude, and the security at any place instantly recognize it. They let her in without complaint. It's all in the attitude. I ask her about it.

"I don't know. I don't even know those guys. But I just act like I belong in here, and they don't hassle me."

"Have you ever been turned away?"

"Rarely. Maybe up in San Diego. You need money to cut a line in San Diego. Down here, it's all how you handle yourself."

Gaby is on a roll now. She loves talking about this stuff.

"Sonia and I used to walk into Frog's with five dollars each," she continues. "We would walk right in, sit down, and wait for some guy to approach us. It was clock-work. We could always find a couple guys to buy us drinks. We used to drink for free. And we never waited in line."

"But a guy is going to expect something in return."

"Maybe, but that wasn't my problem."

The bartender has been listening in on our whole conversation, waiting for us to order. Gaby is very smooth about it, and orders us a *carafe* of the house wine.

I glance at the wine list, and inquire at the bartender, "Do you have a corking fee here?"

"Sí."

"Cuánto?"

"Cien pesos."

Gaby looks at me, "What's a corking fee?"

"If they offer a corking fee," I tell her, "you can bring in your own bottle of wine and they will open it for you and serve."

"That's nice to know. Next time let's bring a bottle."

Casa Plasencia is a Spanish cuisine restaurant-bar, with a bullfighting theme attached. It's a block down from the Agua Caliente Bullring. He brings us the wine, and we order a few tapas. The house wine is always a good choice at Casa Plasencia, and goes down well with the tapas.

"See, it's much easier for women to party every weekend," I tell Gaby, "They don't have to worry about finances. No woman is buying me drinks."

"Sorry, but that's the way it works. We were in Frog's every weekend, and we never had to worry about money. It's nice to not have to worry about it."

"Whatever works, I guess."

"See, now you're catching on. That's the right attitude."

Gaby's order finally arrives. They set three small plates around the table, then provide a small saucer for each of us. This is the way to eat tapas.

"Why do you always order seafood tapas?" I ask Gaby.

"You can never go wrong with mariscos."

"I thought you weren't supposed to eat shrimp at night."

"That's an old wive's tale," she replies. "I can eat mariscos anytime of the day, or night for that matter."

"I agree with the 'old wives'. Seafood doesn't go down well at night. Mariscos is a hot day meal, not a cool evening meal."

"You eat your tapas, and I'll eat mine."

"Fine." I ask the waiter over, and order a tapa of *croquetes de atún* and a plate of *mejillones al ajillo*.

"See, you just ordered tuna and sea mussels," Gaby observes. "That's seafood."

"Doesn't taste like seafood."

"That's because the tuna is fried, and the mussels are in a sauce."

"Well, if I can't beat you, I might as well join you."

"That's the spirit."

The waiter brings my plates. The *croquetes de atún* are served on a hot caste-iron plate. We enjoy our meal, then argue over what to do next. Gaby scans the room, but for once doesn't spot anybody she knows. I consider it a good omen. The food and the wine slows me down, and Gaby seems mellow enough. Gaby is in good spirits, and so am I. A meal in the Zona Rio is always pleasant.

IV

Working bar-back at "Diamond Bill's" is always a trial for me. Every day, I have to work myself up to clock in. I have to convince myself that I need this, and that this is my best option right now. It's all work and little pay. The bar has a unique clientele, but they do tip well. I look outside and see a civic worker trying to light up an old kerosene lamp on the corner of the street. The Gaslamp Quarter in downtown San Diego is dotted with them. It used to be the big scene in San Diego, but it has been taken over by the people of Los Angeles. The vibe is always different. L.A. doesn't have a place like 'Gaslamp', where there is a concentration of clubs and bars. Everything in L.A. is spread out. San Diego provides a concentrated social scene, and they always make a weekend out of it. I can't stand the L.A. crowd. They are too pretentious. Downtown San Diego used to be great; when I first turned twenty-one it was the place to be. Not anymore. Most San Diegans have moved on to other locations, such as North Park and Golden Hills. You will find most San Diegans there. Gaslamp now consists of young men and women dressed to the hilt. The women wear the skimpiest dresses they can find. It's a big competition between all the women on who can look like the biggest whore. All the guys spend way too much time at the gym. You are there to see and be seen. To them, it's all about the club. Too bad the clubs and bars have a last call; about one–thirty in the morning. I'm barely warming up at one–thirty. Also, the restaurants are ridiculously expensive. A good night out in Gaslamp now can run you a couple hundred dollars. I'm not interested in that. If you are in from out of town, it's great. You can have a lot of fun. But for me, who knew Gaslamp before its transformation, it's a big disappointment. I go there to work. The people that visit Gaslamp are there to look good. I'm not interested in that, either.

The good thing about bar-backing is that you stay busy, so the work shift goes by quickly. I'm there to get in and out. Collect my paycheck, and move on. Let the bartenders deal with the annoying drunks, with their sunglasses on at eleven at night. They can't take them off. It can be night time, and they can't take them off. They look ridiculous, but they are surrounded by the same minded people, so they don't care. In a room full of idiots, only the intelligent look stupid. I avoid conversations unless it is necessary. However, that is a detriment in my line of work. An outgoing bartender is a well paid bartender. I need to cultivate that skill to succeed in my chosen trade. A good bartender knows how to work a client. Mixing drinks and pouring a good stout is only part of the equation. Your listening skills have to be superb. It's something I need to work on. My co-workers are alright, but I keep it professional. No need to know.

I clock in at six in the afternoon, and the night goes by quickly. On a Saturday night there are plenty of people out and about in downtown San Diego. The bar is busy. By the time I look up, it's already one in the morning. No need for a lunch or a break. If I need a drink I grab one. If I need to use the bathroom I sneak in and out. There's too much work, but that's the way I like it. I don't bother about a lunch break because I don't want a lunch break. It slows my night down. I want my work shift to fly by. So, I clock in and immediately get busy. My coworkers appreciate my work ethic. They just don't know my motivation. If they did, I wonder if it would alter their perception of me. I delve into my job. By the time I know it, all the patrons have been kicked out and it's just the bartenders and myself cleaning up for the night.

"Evan, what do you do with yourself? I never see you down here, on your own."

"I'm mostly down in TJ."

"TJ? I stopped partying down there when I turned twenty-one."

That's the typical response from people in Southern California. When they turn twenty-one, the party is over south of the border. It's that three year waiting period that the United States forces them to go through. The twenty-one age limit for consuming alcohol is ridiculous. No other country on this planet has a drinking age that late, unless it's a Muslim country and they outlaw alcohol all together.

If you can catch a bullet for your country, you should be able to have a beer in peace.

"I know," I tell him. "I like it down there. A little more freedom. Room to maneuver."

"And dangerous. That's why I stopped going. It's safer to party up here."

"I'm not worried about that. I haven't had trouble, anyway."

Another bartender, Rick, has been listening in.

"Where do you go down there?"

"Oh, most of the dives. I'm not a big clubber, if that's what you mean."

"Where? I used to live in Tijuana," Rick tells me. "You guys still hit up Dandy's?"

"Yeah, or this other bar, the Zacazonapan," I say.

"Never heard of it."

"Most people haven't."

"I wouldn't mind going back down. It's been a few years."

"Anytime. I'll take you down."

"What do you say, Jeff?" Rick asks. "Let's make a trip down to TJ."

"Oh, I don't do TJ. You never know down there, man," Jeff replies.

And there it is, the modern attitude towards south of the border. Maybe it's better for Tijuana, in the long run. Stop marketing and catering to people north of the border. Focus on your own.

"I'll go down with you sometime, Evan. I would be interested," Rick says. "Just take care of me."

"Don't worry, baby, I'll take good care of you alright. And there's no last call down there. Drink all night if you want."

Rick turns back to his co-bartender, "See Jeff, no last call. That's what it's all about." Jeff shakes his head. There's no use trying to convince this guy.

"Last call exists for a reason," Jeff replies. "You need to cut off the drunks before things get out of hand."

I ignore that dumb bastard. Jeff can grate on my nerves, and he can do it in one sentence. He belongs up here.

"Rick, let me know when you want to party with the big boys," I tell him.

Jeff stares at me after that comment. "The real party is up here. Don't go down there Rick. Tijuana is second-rate."

"No place is first-rate with a one–thirty last call," I tell him. "That's ridiculous. Most people in Tijuana don't even hit the bars until midnight."

"Whatever." Jeff dismisses me with a wave of his hand. I turn to Rick and give him the real details on Tijuana.

"Yeah, but I can't get too crazy," Rick tells me. "The wife and kids, you know."

It's hard to peel off native San Diegans. Life is too good up here. Why take a chance? That's the attitude north of the border. Five, ten years ago, plenty of Americans were perfectly willing to go to Tijuana to party and carry on. There used to be a 'College Night' in Tijuana. It was always Wednesday night. All the underage college girls from San Diego and Los Angeles would roll on down to the noisy discothèques on La Revu. Not anymore. It's not worth the hassle to travel south of the border, unless it is Cancun or a Cruise. That's the modern attitude. Very well.

"Evan, you finished yet?"

"Just about."

"Ok, when you finish washing, polish up the bar, then we can leave."

Rick leans over and hands me two twenty dollar bills—"tips." He doesn't have to do that, but he does. I like Rick; he's a good guy. Jeff is fine to work with. However, I could hang out with Rick. Rick always kicks in a percentage of his tips to the bar-back. Jeff rarely does. It's really up to the bartender. I enjoy working with Rick. But Rick's already locked in, so I doubt he will ever take me up on my offer. Jeff I wouldn't even bother about.

"Evan, what about your girl? What's her name?"

"Gabriela."

"She seems pretty nice," Rick tells me. "Smart girl. You should lock down a woman like that."

"I'm trying."

They laugh at that one.

"Evan, you ever going to settle down?" Jeff asks.

"If I get around to it."

Rick looks at Jeff, and they start arguing over whether I should settle down or not. Jeff supports it. Rick is against it.

"You can have a wife and still have fun," Jeff says.

"No you can't," Rick argues. "Once you get married and have kids, everything changes."

"Evan, get married. It will stabilize your life."

"Evan, don't get married. Definitely don't have kids, yet. At least not until you're forty. You can never go back."

I shake my head at these two. Jeff and Rick are two different sides of the same, scarred coin. Well, I'm not playing either game.

"Don't worry, Rick, I have no intention of either."

"That's my boy."

"Evan, you life is going to pass you by," Jeff says.

"Let it. At least he will enjoy it," Rick replies.

Rick is a good guy. He's overweight, and not the best looking guy in the world, but he can get along with anybody. He's smart about the way he dresses, and he hides his weight well. Some over-weight people dress well, others don't. Rick is smart about it. He trims twenty pounds off of his figure by the way he dresses. He is always well dressed. Not expensively dressed, but well dressed. There's a difference. His wife is gorgeous. I'm always proud of Rick for getting a girl like that. Marissa, his wife, is damned beautiful. I kick myself for missing a woman like that. Good for Rick, though. Rick is outgoing. Women love talking to him. He can work a good tip out of the stingiest customers. Jeff is the opposite. He is trim, cut, and classically handsome. He can only get tips out of people similar to himself. His clients have to share the same bourgeois attitude that he does. Then, he can get along. If you come in looking like a bum or a punk, you might get a cold shoulder from Jeff. He's damn good looking, though. His wife is the same. He has two children, girls, and they look the same. They all have lifetime memberships to their local gym. The perfect life. Jeff is always complaining about his work hours, but in his profession all the money is made at night. I think he has management aspirations, though. With Jeff, I would believe it. He has 'Shift Manager' written all over him.

I lean over to Rick and whisper, "Anytime you want to come down with me, you're invited. Bring your wife along. I'll show you a good time, and no trouble. I promise."

I can tell Rick wants to go. He's not paying me lip service.

"I'll ask her."

"You do that."

I finish up my work, excuse myself, and leave for the night. I hop onto the highway and enjoy the drive with my window down. It's a warm summer's night and I can drive on the highway with the window down and not be cold. There is nobody on the highway at this time of the night except for a few inebriated drivers and the occasional patrol car looking for his next victim. I drive down to my house, but I stop by the local taco shop. Taco shops in San Diego are different than the ones in Tijuana. Here, it's greasy food served with flour tortillas. There is Mexican food, then there is 'American' Mexican food. There is a difference. The American variety is prepared differently: more grease, more meat, and more calories. You can put on some major pounds by sticking to a Mexican food diet up in the United States.

I feel like a big burrito, to settle me down for the rest of the night. Greasy food can knock you right out. The taco shop is crowded, full of San Diegans kicked out of their bars after 'last call'. It's two–thirty in the morning. I eat my burrito by myself, trying to catch the conversation at the table next to me. It's three guys and two girls, all drunk. The guys are trying to figure out who is going to go home with whom. The girls seem willing. They will string the guys out for a while, I guess. The same scene is playing out all over the tiny restaurant. Men with women, and men without women. That's the name of the game. Everybody is too loud. They all shout at each other, even though they are two feet away from each other. Every guy has a dress shirt, perfectly pressed. The top three buttons are undone, exposing their chests. The girls all have skirts that are too short for them. The guys wear more jewelry than the girls. I can't stand these people. In Holden Caulfield's own words, they are a bunch of 'phonies', all of them. One guy gets up from his chair to shout at one of his friends. They keep up a conversation this way. He seems very excited. His conversation consists of violent hand gestures, to emphasize whatever mindless point he is trying to make. Many Americans get excited when they talk. It appears that a real conversation is stimulating, as opposed to communicating with technology, so when they find themselves communicating with a live person rather than an inanimate object, they get overly excited. They need the excitement. He is waving his hands all over the place. I can follow the whole conversation by his hand gestures alone. Then his partner stands up and gets animated. They look like they are about to get into fight, but they don't. It's a friendly conversation. I'm convinced that most Americans are going hard of hearing. It's the way they scream at each other.

I'm getting tired of listening to the noise around me, so it's back home and back to bed. I need to save up some money, so I try to keep my expenses down. I want to enjoy myself this summer, but you need money to do that. Partying here, or anywhere in California, is prohibitively expensive. I avoid it. I can get twice the value for my dollar south of the border. I need to call Jake tomorrow, to see if there is any work on that end. It would be nice at this point to have a cell phone, but I won't go there, yet. I'll just have to call him from my house tomorrow morning to see if he needs anything.

V

There are many ways to make money on the border. Some pay more than others. Some are more dangerous than others. My racket is steroids. Easier to cross, less dangerous, and if caught you just pay a fine. I have a friend who body-builds, and there is a large market for anabolics. It's easy to pick up as well. These guys actually use steroids designated for horses. Horse steroids. Insane. People look up to body-builders as men and women who are in shape. Who are healthy. My friend Jake, who is a body-builder, once told me, "It's not about being healthy. It's about looking healthy." I believe him.

I'm crossing into San Diego with a friend today. We meet down in Tijuana, pick up our stash, and return to the border crossing. I usually like to cross with a partner; I believe it attracts less attention. My buddy, Gerardo Sanchez, seems a bit skittish about this. Maybe Gerardo was the wrong idea. Next time, I think I'll ask Adrian. Gaby wanted me to find him something, so here it is. I don't know why she doesn't use her vaunted connections down here, but I think about it and Adrian is an American Citizen, so he can't work down here. I guess it's up to me. I have my issues with Adrian, but Gerardo worries me. He's a little too nervous.

"What happens if they catch us? I'm not going to jail for a pocket full of pills. I'm going to walk a few people behind you."

"Relax," I tell him. "I never get caught. Just act normal; pretend you're spending a pleasant day in Tijuana. Besides, you won't go to jail for this stuff. It's like crossing cigars."

"No, it's not like cigars. They just confiscate the cigars. 'Roids are illegal. It's like crossing drugs."

"No, it's not like crossing drugs. I have them in prescription bottles, and the prescription says something else. If they catch me, I just say they're antibiotics and they take them."

"They don't test them?" Gerardo asks me. I thought about that. Nobody ever asked me that question.

"I don't know. Like I said: I've never been caught."

"They're still drugs, though," he says. "Who do you sell them to?"

"Jake. You know Jake, the big guy. Body-builder. Anyway, it's not like I'm crossing heroin or coke. I'm not contributing to anyone's unhappiness. I'm not peddling in anyone's misery."

"If that makes you sleep better at night. But 'Roids can fuck up a guy pretty bad as well."

"Yeah, but they're not addictive. And it's not like they're going to use them the rest of their lives. They just need them before competitions."

"Alright."

"Actually, it used to be pretty exciting," I explain to him. "I used to feel great after I got across. The payoff was almost secondary. It's just the feeling of doing something you're not supposed to be doing. I think I got started on this because I was bored. I don't know, I can't explain it."

The truth is I need the extra cash. I can't support my lifestyle working bar-back all of the time. It's a straight wage job. I don't share the tips with the bartenders. Those greedy bastards hold out on me. Other than Rick, I rarely get in on the tips. Bar backing doesn't make the nut. And of course the hours suck. They are horrible, and on top of that I refuse to work every weekend. My bosses are frequently angered at that, but I stick to my guns. I need my weekends. I have lost a job or two because of it, but I don't care. I just wish I could make more money. Bar-backing is really just doing the dirty work for a bartender, and while you do it you are supposed to be learning the trade.

My problem is I refuse to work in an office with nine-to-five hours. I just can't do it. I've never been a nine-to-five guy. I can't walk into work every day with a suit and tie. Clock-in and clock-out; make sure you take your lunch, but don't take too long. To hell with that. I need variability in my work schedule. I can't handle regimentation. Bar backing fits that, but the pay isn't great. I can't keep up with Gaby and my friends with that wage. I need to supplement my income. As I said, there are plenty of opportunities on the border for a man looking for additional income.

We get in line and at the customs area. It's pretty routine here. Tourists out for the day. Japanese, Chinese, European, all mixed in with the locals getting across for a day's work in San Diego. That is pretty much the border line, tourists mingled in with the working class folks. The line is great right now. We only make about ten minutes. I have seen the pedestrian line all the way back into Colonia Libertad. There, on certain days, you can wait standing up in line for three hours or more. I've seen people pass out from the heat just from standing straight for a couple hours. But the line is moving pretty quick today. I pull out my driver's license and get ready. I scout out the inspector, and he is an over-weight middle-aged white man. His stomach is spilling out over his utility belt. I thought U.S. Customs Agents had physical fitness standards, but maybe this guy is grand-fathered in. He looks bored, which is just the type of attitude I'm looking for. There are two standard questions any inspector will ask.

"Citizenship?"

"U.S."

"Anything from Mexico?"

"Nothing."

He waves me through. Easy. I appear to be an upstanding young gentleman from the U.S., out for a day in Mexico. As I'm walking out of the area, I notice Gerardo is held up. They might send him to secondary inspection. The biggest thing is attitude. If you act bored, like you have done this a thousand times, they won't give you a second look. But Gerardo was nervous, and he didn't even have anything, other that a vial of pills stuffed in his pocket. I just brought him along to appear less conspicuous, and maybe he could become a partner of sorts. I want to see if Gerardo is the right man for the job. That's the thing. Usually these customs inspectors are pretty much drones, ushering the line along, but they are trained to look for certain things. What you wear, your general appearance, accent, so forth. If they detect anything out of the ordinary, off to secondary you go. Gerardo has no worries though, because he has nothing on him other than 'prescription' medications. They most they can do is bust him for not declaring them. I used to get a rush after I made it across, but not much anymore. Maybe I should stop, but I am getting pretty good at it now. I pat the pill vials in my coat pocket. This isn't much, just to supplement the income a little. It's very easy to make a dollar on the border if you have good nerves and the right attitude.

* * * *

As soon as we get across I meet Jake at a restaurant close to the border. I ask Gerardo to wait outside for me while I speak to Jake. Jake informs me that he needs another haul.

"Big competition coming up. A lot of guys are in demand right now."

"Aren't you competing against these guys? Why do you want to supply them?"

"All in the spirit of competition," Jake informs me. "We don't consider steroid use as cheating. It's all part of the game."

Whatever. Explain that to the Baseball people. Body-builders are an eccentric group of individuals. I don't know that world, and I don't want to know that world. Jake is an old friend; we knew each other before he got into the body-building lifestyle. I try not to get involved. He's invited me to a few events, but I always decline. I have no interest in that. It's a small community, not one I want to be part of. I try not to judge my friends on how they make their living— I'm not one to judge. Unless it is grossly unethical, I don't bother them, as long as they don't bother me. If Jake needs my help, I give him my help. And I make my profit on the wayside.

"So, how much do you need this time?" I ask him.

"Just triple the amount. We need the same stuff: Some 'Clen', some 'Deca', and give me a few thousand milligrams of 'Dianabol.' I got about four guys asking me for the juice. They will pay premium, but it better be the real deal."

"You can't get bigger than Deca. That stuff will buck up a horse."

Deca-Durabolin, or 'Deca,' is the real deal for steroid enthusiasts. It can put weight on anybody, with minimal side effects. It's designed to put muscle mass on horses, so on a human being it will do the trick. Jake always loads up a few weeks before a competition. Deca-Durabolin is diffi-cult to get, but I have the right connections. 'Clen,' or Clenbuterol, is not an Anabolic. Clen gets rid of fat, so Body builders will load up on Clen before a competition. It really tones them up. You won't put any weight on with

Clen though, it's just used to drop your body fat ratio and sharpen those muscles.

The 'Dianabol' order throws me for a loop. Jake rarely throws in an order for Dianabol. D-bol is the old stuff; one of the original Anabolic Steroids. D-bol is a classic steroid, the one the old Olympic athletes were using before people caught on. You can put on serious muscle mass with D-bol, but with nasty side effects. Blood pressure can go up, estrogen levels will increase, testicles will shrink—the whole nine yards. All the evil stereotypes and innuendo surrounding steroid use is probably attributed to D-bol. It's been around since the sixties. Dianabol is dangerous. Everything has a price south of the border, and I usually mark up about fifty percent or so. It's good profit, so I don't pass it down. Jake has never crossed down to Tijuana. He's afraid. That works to my advantage.

I look through the window at Gerardo and he still seems nervous. This type of work is not for him. Too bad, because I like Gerardo. He would have made a great partner.

I automatically scratch Gerardo off of my list. I won't cross with him again. He is an occupational hazard. I'll give Adrian a call. He should be up for this type of work. He's a worse scoundrel than me, so he should fit right in.

"Evan, but I need this stuff quickly. Like today, or tomorrow."

"Wow. Ok, let me get set up. I have another guy I can call."

I walk out and dismiss Gerardo. We agree to get together next week for some beers, but it's one of those plans that never fall through. You know when you make real plans with somebody, and when you are paying lip service. Gerardo and I both know we are paying each other lip service, but we respect each other as friends, so we keep up the façade. It's important, because I value my friends. Gerardo Sanchez is a good friend; just not the type of friend for this work. I don't always get along with Adrian, but this is a business decision. I immediately call Adrian and tell him I need some help, and that he can make some money doing it.

* * * *

The next afternoon I meet Adrian Mora at a taco stand in downtown Tijuana on the corner of Boulevard Sánchez-Taboada and Calle Ocho. The place is called Tacos *El Franc* or Tacos *Francais*, depending on who you ask. Tacos *El Franc* is quite possibly the best taco stand in Tijuana, and that's saying something. Corn tortillas, carne asada, adobada, tripas, cabeza lengua, all of it. In a true Tijuana taco stand, they use the whole cow. Carne asada–your typical meat. Adobada–pork. Tripa–cow intestines. Cabeza–cow brains. Lengua–cow tongue. The list goes on and on.

I don't know what I want so I ask Adrian what he eats here.

"The adobada is good, but I always go for the tripa. That's the best taco in Tijuana, right there. Tacos de tripa."

"I've never had cow intestine before, but what the hell. I'll give it a shot."

I order two tacos de 'tripa' and two de 'adobada.' Adobada is a favorite of mine. The red-orange meat is cooked on a slow upright rotisserie. On top of the rotisserie is a pineapple. The open flame is on one side of the rotisserie, heating the meat as it turns. The taquero stands on the opposite side of the flame, shaving off the meat as it rotates. You can feel the heat from the flame as you stand by and order. The pineapple drips off into the meat as it is cooked. It adds an extra dimension to the flavor. Always look for the pineapple on top of the rotisserie when you order adobada. It has the ring of authenticity; you know the *taquero* is doing something right when that pineapple sits on top. They shave off the meat as needed to fill tacos. Great stuff. The 'tripa' is interesting. The meat is very tender. It stands in good contrast to the adobada , which is strong and flavorful. Great combination.

"Alright, so what's the plan?" Adrian asks me.

"We can leave anytime now. It should be late enough. Inspectors don't hassle much at this time of the evening. They'll just figure us to be a couple of kids back from a party. The will wave us right through."

"Sounds good. By the way, thanks for the work. My financial aide doesn't come in for another few weeks, so I'm a little short right now."

"You're still in school?" I ask.

"No, I already dropped out, but late enough to collect my check. I'll get paid soon."

"Why not get a real job?"

"What? No way. I'm not a working stiff like you. It's much easier this way. I just get paid to go to school."

"But you don't go to school. You dropped out."

"No, sometimes I finish a semester, sometimes I don't. I get paid the same anyway."

"Must be nice," I say.

"It is. You should go back to school. Get in on it."

Adrian approached me a few weeks back asking me if there was any work. Then Gaby bugged me about it. As I said, there's always work on the border for someone looking for it. Gerardo wasn't working out. I don't want to get caught with a shaky partner. Jake needs a good haul, so I recruited Adrian. I need an extra set of hands because it's too much product for me to cross by myself. I can't claim nasal decongestant with that much. It will draw suspicion. Adrian can help. He's fine for the work. He once had to cross a guy back illegally in his car. No problems there. The person in question was actually was a legal resident of Los Angeles. The problem is when you are applying for U.S. citizenship you can't leave the country unless expressly permitted. To get that permission takes weeks, if not months. This guy had a mother who had a heart-attack back in Mexico. He couldn't wait for the U.S. Government to get around to giving him permission to leave the country, so he just left on a whim. He ran his own business in Los Angeles and everything: a very upstanding gentleman. Problem was, he needed to return to Los Angeles after he made arrangements for his mother. Of course he couldn't cross by legal channels. So, he asked Adrian to cross him. No problem. He told Adrian he would pay five hundred dollars to do it, then another two hundred to drive him to Los Angeles. Adrian said 'yes'. The guy spoke perfect English. He sat in the passenger seat anyway, and when you cross they normally question the driver only. He never drew attention to himself. Good business opportunity, right here on the border.

"This will be a little different than crossing your pal," I inform Adrian. "You could have claimed ignorance there. Just said, 'Officer, I had no idea this guy was illegal. He's a friend of my father's.' That's not going to work here."

Adrian laughs, "I'll just say, 'Officer, what do you mean, 'Steroids?' My friend over there who crossed with me told me they were decongestants. You might want to talk to him.'"

We both laughed at that one. I told him that might work, if I wasn't crossing 'medication' as well.

"Don't say decongestant. That contains Sudafren. They will think we are tweakers, out to stew our own batch. Say cough suppressant, or antibiotic."

"Doesn't cough suppressants contain codine? Now we're getting high."

"Alright, fuck them both. Just say they're Tylenol, because we have headaches."

Adrian looks at me, and I can tell he's not entirely convinced.

"Ok, here's what I will do. You can cross the Clen. This stuff is not technically a Steroid."

"Then what is it?"

"Have you ever heard of Albuterol?"

"Oh, yeah. The medication for Asthma."

"That's right. This right here is called Clenbuterol. It's in the same family as Albuterol. If worse gets to worst, just tell them you have Asthma medication."

"Why do body-builders want Asthma medication?" Adrian asks me.

"They don't. Clen works a little differently. It breaks down fat tissue. They don't put on weight with this stuff, but they get ripped. It also disguises other steroids. When they test, the Clen can mask the other steroids."

Adrian looks down at the bottle, "Shoot, I should start using this stuff."

The later you cross the better. Eleven at night is the perfect time to cross the border. The clubbers and ravers and bar hoppers in Tijuana are barely walking out the door, so they are not crossing yet. No commuters at that time either. The Tijuana housewives out for a day of shopping at the San Diego malls are home asleep at that hour. The problem is Adrian and I have to kill a few hours down here to make it to eleven o'clock. We'll have to find a few distractions.

"Who's picking us up?"

"We're supposed to meet Jake at a restaurant right across the border. He should be there waiting for us."

"He'll pay us right there?"

"Yeah. Don't worry, he's good for the money."

Adrian looks at me, "Any way to make more?"

"What do you mean?"

Sure, there was plenty of ways to make more money at the border, but much more dangerous.

I order two more tacos. I'm hungry. This time, I order tacos de lengua. Cow-tongue tacos.

"You don't cross anything else?" he asks again.

"Nope. This pays just fine," I tell him. "Don't get greedy, man. That's how criminals always get caught. You get too greedy, then they pop you. Believe me, you don't want to get stuck for crossing drugs. Federal crime. Mandatory minimum sentences. I knew a guy who got caught crossing smack. No priors, nothing. Not even a speeding ticket to his name. Five years, minimum. No thanks."

"How about crossing heads?"

"That's pays alright; better than this. But it's very easy to get caught. That's what they catch the most. And you're going to need a modified car to do that. They have to modify it. Or you can drive one of theirs, but your cut won't be as big then."

"What happens if you get caught crossing heads?"

"Depends. You have to be careful. A lot of times, you don't even see the car being prepared, or packed. If the people don't have proper ventilation or something, you get hit with a few more felonies. Reckless endangerment. It happened to Ramon. Remember Ramon Villegas? He thought he was crossing a few heads in his trunk, but what he didn't know hurt him. They also stashed a person in the engine block. Bad move, but he didn't know about it. He wasn't around when they prepared the car. So when they pulled this guy out of the engine block, Ramon got hit with another felony."

"Why?"

"A few immigrants have died that way. Of course it's dangerous to stash somebody in an engine block. Those guys don't care; they just care about the money. They might stash a kid in the engine block for all you know. The authorities might charge you with negligence, or attempted man-slaughter. They were more lenient before, but now they're cracking down."

It can get tricky crossing people that way, so I never bother. They can also stash drugs in your car, without you knowing. The protocol is to pick up a car that has been already prepared, then just drive across. Most people have no clue how many people they are crossing, or how they were packed in. I've seen it happen all the time. Some poor fool thinks he's crossing heads for one hundred bucks a person, then when he gets caught he finds out they packed the door panels with Marijuana as well. Tack on a few extra felonies for that one, and pleading ignorance won't help. On top of it, if they pack in the people wrong, you can be charged with reckless endangerment as well. Too many variables for me. I stick with the pills.

"So, how are things with Gaby? Made any progress?"

"Ok., I guess. Why so interested?"

"No, just wondering. I've known Gaby longer than you, that's all. I know how she can be."

I wonder what he means by that. Adrian is never curious for no good reason. That he has to throw in that he knows Gaby better than I do bothers me. Maybe it wasn't such a good idea to bring him along. He's probably after her. Adrian is a straight womanizer. I give him credit though; he barely has to work at it. I've never seen women attracted to a guy like that. I have seen perfectly fine women come right up to him and hit on him. It's damn peculiar. He can put in minimal effort and still get his action. I feel sorry for Sonia, Gaby's cousin. Either she's clueless, or knows about it and ignores it. Maybe she thinks it's idle flirting. Too bad, because I respect Sonia. She's a great woman. Adrian is wrong for her. I don't totally blame Adrian, though. If women were throwing themselves at me they way they throw themselves at him, I would probably be womanizing as well. It would be too easy. You couldn't say no. Adrian can get women at his leisure, and I'm talking any type of women. Older women, younger women, good looking women, strange looking women. I've seen them all pretty much offer themselves up to this guy. He's not the type to turn them down. The fact that he asked about Gaby puts that seed of doubt in my mind. I worry about it. Adrian seems keenly interested in my racket though, and needles me with questions.

"Just be careful you're not wasting too much time with her," he tells me. "She'll play games, man. I've seen her play plenty of guys. That's how she operates."

"Don't worry about me. I can take care of myself. Just worry right now about getting across."

That seemed to take some air out of his head. It's his simpering composure that gets to me.

"They have cracked down lately, sending more people to secondary," I tell him.

"9/11?"

"Yep. 9/11. You won't go to jail the first time you get caught crossing heads, but you're bound to get caught soon. Like I said, that's the easiest one to get caught in. If they don't rig the car right, or they pop your hood or trunk, that's it. Game over."

"We'll see."

"Are you ready?" I ask Adrian.

"Sure, let go."

"I want to make a quick pit-stop before we head over to the Pharmacy."

"Alright, let's get going.

We add up our tacos and pay the bill. Then we head down the street towards downtown Tijuana. We stop by an

Oxxo and purchase a couple of beers on our way over. They clerk gives us each a brown bag for our beer so we can drink on the street while we walk.

With our concealed beers in hand, we stroll over to Calle Sexta and observe all the bars and clubs preparing for the night. Delivery men are dropping off crates of beer and liquor. Employees are cleaning and mopping up their establishments, getting ready for the night. They water down the sidewalk and push all of the trash in the gutter and down the storm-drain. We look inside the bars to see if any of them are open. Adrian suggests we take a seat inside, but I have a few priorities.

First, I want to walk over to the *Ciruela Electrica*, a music store situated between Avenida Revolución and Constitución. The always have an eclectic choice of music; whatever the owner can get his hands on. There's another music store right next to it, but they sell mostly Heavy Metal and Industrial music. The "Electric Plum" sells just about everything else. It's a small store, with a Jimi Hendrix psychedelic looking sign hanging over the establishment. I always like walking in there because I never know what I'm looking for, but I always find something good. I can walk out of there with a cd I've never seen before, but something I want to hear. Spontaneity is a great thing. The "Electric Plum" has it. It's a small record store, right on Calle Sexta, south of La Revu. It's an easy walk for us. Adrian is a big music buff, so he doesn't mind walking over with me.

"This place has been open for years. I love this store."

"Me too. You can even find some good vinyl in here."

"I know. I found some great Pink Floyd vinyl in here the other day," I say. "Shoot, they even sell tapes in here."

"I haven't bought a tape in years."

"Me neither. But they have them in there."

It's a subject that Adrian and I agree on. I might not always get along with Adrian, but we can always agree on good music. I size up a man by his taste in music. Adrian has good taste in music. He can listen to anything, and he has even pointed me in the right direction a few times.

The good thing about music stores is that they carry flyers for shows coming up all over the city. That's part of the experience: 'Let's see who's playing in Tijuana this month.' There are a couple good shows I would be interested in. I grab a few flyers and put them in my pocket. When you walk into a good music store you are walking into a time-warp. They still exist in Tijuana. Cd's, vinyl, and tapes are stacked and labeled all around us. Dust-covered music posters dot the walls. The place feels old. Adrian is looking through the cd's, and he grabs one. Good. It's better when we cross that we appear to be real tourists. It will attract less attention. I should buy something too. I grab a cd, by a band called 'Natiruts', from Brazil. They are a fusion band: Reggae and Jazz. I'm surprised to find this cd here; they can be difficult to find. You can only purchase their stuff online. They play great music, but they are not well known outside of Brazil. This is why I like coming here. I had no idea I was going to end up buying a 'Natiruts' cd, but here I am with one in my hand. I haven't seen this cd before either, so hopefully it's new music. Adrian and I complete our transactions, and with bags in hand we hail a cab and make our way to the pharmacy, then the border. Time to get to work, and then, hopefully, get paid.

* * * *

I told Adrian a trip down to Tijuana is always worth it; if nothing else we had the opportunity to visit the record shop. He agrees. We talk about this as we ride in our cab down to the border. Our cab driver is listening in, and recommends another good music store. We confide in him that we are a pair of audiophiles, and are always on the lookout for any obscure record shop. He agrees. If you ever want the low-down on whatever strange city you find yourself in, jump in a cab and pick the driver's brains. More often than not, they can be a treasure trove of information. This guy fits the bill. His name is Rafael, or Rafa, and he has been driving a cab for a few years now. Before that he was a Tijuana Municipal cop, but things got a little crazy for him and driving a cab pays better, he tells us. However, his previous employment affords him a few opportunities as a taxi driver; the cops know who he is, and they leave him alone. Adrian tells him, "that's magic" as far as a cab driver is concerned, and I agree. Intimate knowledge of the local police force can be advantageous to anybody that makes his living on the road. His former life as a Tijuana beat cop is the perfect qualification. When we exit his cab at the border, I make sure to write his name and number down. He tells us to give him a call anytime we're down here, and if he's available he can pick us up. I tell him I don't mind paying a few extra pesos for a cab I can trust and that knows the city better than I do. I put his number straight in my wallet.

Unlike Gerardo, Adrian isn't bothered by the scene here, and by the fact that he possesses a certain quantity of illegal steroids in his pocket. As I said, Adrian knows the score here.

"When do we meet your friend for the drop-off? I've got plans later."

"As soon as we cross. Jake will be waiting for us. They have a big competition coming up, and a few guys really need this stuff," I tell him.

"Good. It's nice to work and get paid on the same day."

"Yes, it is."

As we wait in line, I look around to see if I recognize any of the inspectors I saw on the last cross. No need for those uniforms to put two-and-two together. Adrian is right behind me, smoking a cigarette. I tell him to put it out. This isn't Tijuana anymore. Smoking in here is illegal. He agrees, and puts it out. That was dangerous. The line is moving quickly, which is a good sign for us. That means they are waving people right through. I scout ahead, but this time it's an Asian-looking inspector, and he sits and stares at everybody's passport for a few seconds before letting them through. When it's my turn, I stroll up to the booth, and I get into my script.

"Citizenship?"

"U.S."

"Bringing anything from Mexico?"

"Nothing."

He stares at me for a second, glances at my passport, contemplates his decision, then waves me through. The Asian inspectors always make a big scene about letting anybody through. I get the feeling they enjoy keeping people on the hook for a second or two before they let you pass. Adrian is speaking to the inspector in the next booth. I walk through, slowly, waiting for Adrian to catch up. I want to stop and turn around, but I don't. Not with a few hundred dollars worth of drugs in my pocket. I keep walking, slowly. Nothing. I spare a quick glance over my shoulder and see Adrian still in a deep conversation with the inspector. Another one approaches from behind. Now they are both talking to him. Suddenly an officer notices me lingering and walks up to me.

"You need to move on," the Inspector informs me. "Are you waiting for somebody? Are you with that guy?"

He points to Adrian and the two inspectors.

"No," I reply. 'Trouble,' I think. He could have seen Adrian and myself walking across together. One too many lies. I make my way towards the door. Once I get outside, I try to look in, but the glass is tinted. I walk over to the trolley station, and I sit down on a bench. Adrian doesn't emerge. A minute passes. Then two minutes. Suddenly, it occurs to me that this was a bad idea. If Adrian gets caught, this will get back to Gaby and Sonia in no time. Then the game will really be up. Suddenly, I see a commotion off to the side of the station. Customs officers are running towards the car line. Sirens sound off, and people are running everywhere. The only thing that crosses my mind is Adrian. I should probably leave now. If Adrian is caught, they might implicate me as well. I don't want to get caught because I was sitting here like an idiot. I feel bad; I don't want to abandon Adrian. But if he is caught, there is nothing I can do loitering around here. I don't know what to do. I stand up, purchase a Trolley ticket, and immediately hop on the Red Trolley that was waiting there. The doors slam shut with hydraulic force, and it starts its journey north into San Diego, and safety. Gaby and Sonia, more than Adrian, jump in my mind. This time, it looks like I'm going to get caught. I would rather it be by Customs than by Adrian.

A cell phone would be handy now, but I don't have one. As soon as I see Jake, I'll borrow his and try to give Adrian a call. Hopefully everything is alright. This evening turned dangerous in a hurry.

VI

A night in Tijuana is always a good idea, so a few friends and I agree to get together and go for a 'walk.' A walk, for us, is a bar-hop, all through Tijuana. Centro de Tijuana is made for this. Many of the best bars in downtown are within walking distance, and it's safe enough. Tijuana makes an honest effort at keeping this part of town safe for pedestrians. It benefits us, so we decide on a downtown stroll. The good thing about Adrian is that he is always game for a good bar-hop through Tijuana. He's the first one to agree to it. Also, I'm keen on speaking with him. I haven't seen him since we crossed yesterday, but Gaby told me through Sonia that he made it across after all. I want to hear his story, and find out where his product is. There is still profit to be made. So we all agree to meet at a bar called "Monte Carlo", then start from there.

The "Monte Carlo" is a working class bar right next door to a mechanic's shop. Downtown Tijuana, or "Centro", isn't as glamorous as the Zona Rio, and the main Ave-nue, Revolución, is a bit gaudy. The "Monte Carlo" is a few blocks from La Revu so it's nestled in an industrial area. You wouldn't think a bar would exist here, but they do pretty steady business. Mostly Tijuaneros during their lunch hour, or after work, stop on by.

Adrian and Ricardo Tellez are the first to arrive. I pick up Israel Duarte and Eduardo Tellez up in San Diego, then we all drive across. Israel Duarte is one of my best friends, and Eduardo and Ricardo Tellez are more Gaby 'cousins.' Eduardo and Ricardo are good guys, though. I've known Ricardo longer than I have known Gaby. Eddie is down for the weekend, and I always include him when I can.

Adrian and Ricardo are into a few drinks already when we arrive. We can catch up, though. Adrian has had a few beers, and he is in the mood for music. He orders a few songs from the 'Trio' outside. Our Trio walk in and I see that they are all old, wrinkled, and their costumes and in-struments appear to be about twenty years old. Typically, these are the best street musicians. The older, the better. They have on silk shirts with a western motif, and their white cowboy hats are sweat stained and yellowing out. These guys are 'veteranos,' and they are always the best mu-sicians.

Adrian beckons them in, tells them what he wants to hear, and they commence playing. The people next to us also get to enjoy, for free. They get to 'hop on' our intimate concert right here in the bar. After they are done, we pay the fellows, then they hit up the other tables and pick up a few more orders for songs. That's how it works down here; you can enjoy a good hour of live music at any establishment in Tijuana if everybody is willing to pay their fair share. Our other patrons this evening are up to the task. The musicians make their way from table to table and play a few songs each, but we all get to enjoy the music. Socialism in action, but with a capitalist bent. They make a decent living this way; cruising around different bars and restaurants offering their services. They can charge about five dollars a song. You can get a discount if you order more. Tijuana is full of such musicians.

I try to make eye contact with Adrian, to see what is going on. I can't mention our business in front of Gaby's cousins, though. Adrian seems to be ignoring me. Everybody else, however, is ready to drink and enjoy themselves.

"A good Mariachi has at least two-hundred songs in their repertoire," Israel Duarte claims.

"By heart," Eduardo agrees.

"Of course. How else do you think they play? They have to know all of their songs."

"It would be bad for any Mariachi or Norteño to take a request and not know the song," Israel says.

"They usually charge by the hour, though."

We finish our drinks, order another round of bottles each, put them in brown bags, and walk with our drinks over to the corner of Revolution and Calle Primera.

Calle Primera is full of musicians tonight. There is maybe sixty to eighty, mixed Maricahi, Norteño, and Trio, all standing around waiting for their clients. The Mariachi are your typical Mexican folk singers, wearing classic black sombreros. Norteños are Mexico's version of Country music singers. They hail from the northern states of Mexico, hence 'Norteños.' Trio is a three-piece band playing romantic or folk songs. They are all there, hanging around the street corner.

"Let's go into the 'Red Dragon' first, before we get back to La Revu."

"What, you want a Cahuama first?"

"I never understood that," Israel states, confused.

"Cahuama?" Ricardo answers. "Literal translation is 'tortoise'; actual meaning is a 32oz of beer—in a bottle. It's fat, hence, 'Cahuama.' "

"Yes, I want a 'Cahuama.' "

We all laughed at that. Israel had a knack for stating the obvious, and a talent for timing. It makes him a valued member of the group. In Joseph Conrad's words, he was 'One of Us.' "

We walk into the bar, and our senses become alert. It's a different scene. We don't blend in here, but hopefully we can become accepted.

"Well, this is the right place. It's fucking cheap."

"That's why I like it."

The Red Dragon is a hold-over from the Prohibition Era. It certainly looks the part. The 'Dragon Rojo' is long, narrow, with a bar running the length and a juke box at the end. A few tables are pushed up against the other side. It has an upstairs balcony with tables overlooking the bar. All of it 'Saloon' style. The whole establishment is bathed is a red light, with a Dragon etched in glass above the bar, hence the name 'Red Dragon'. The juke box makes the place work. A friend of mine once said, "If you break up with your woman, this is the place to be." It is. You will always find the odd Mariachi or two drinking their troubles away at the end of the bar. You can still smoke inside, and you will always find a few dusty old hookers on the other end of the bar, near the entrance, searching for their next drink and the next meal. The Red Dragon is situated between La Coahuila and Revolución, so it is in between both worlds. It is a gateway, from La Coahuila, or to La Coahuila. The Red Dragon is a psychic border, to and from civilization. This time, we are leaving civilization.

Once you pass the Red Dragon heading south, you enter into the 'Tolerance Zone' of Tijuana, referred to as "La Coahuila." 'Coahuila' is actually the name of a street where Adelita's is located, along with a few other brothels. It is the more infamous of 'Calles' compromising the Tolerance Zone, so the whole area is named after it. Honorific, to say the least. Adelita's is synonymous with 'La Coahuila', so the connection exists. Adelita's is also the best brothel in Tijuana. You are practically guaranteed the best looking women in Tijuana there. The bonus is that they are, indeed, women. In Tijuana, the distinction is important. There are many 'establishments' just as popular for their sexually ambiguous employees in Tijuana. Any local will point you in the right, or wrong direction. So you have to be careful.

Walking around "La Coahuila" is an unusual experience for any non-local. And you know once you enter the "Zone." There are prostitutes lining the streets, with plenty of cheap hotels to provide service.

"Hey, how much does it cost for a girl here?" Eddie asks.

"On the street, or in a club?"

"Both."

"You can get laid with any of these girls for about twenty dollars. Inside the clubs, you can grab one for about fifty, sixty bucks," Ricardo informs us.

"Why more expensive inside?"

"Generally, the girls are better looking in the clubs. They won't be guaranteed hookers, though. Some are just dancers, so you have to ask," I inform Eddie.

"What about 'Adelita's?'"

"Oh yeah, they're all prostitutes in there. Pretty good looking, too."

"Yeah," Ricardo states. "You can get the best in there."

"Shoot, that place probably started 'La Coahuila.' "

"Yeah, Adelita's isn't really a strip club though. It's a straight brothel. All of the women are available."

"Oh, ok."

"The other strip clubs, it depends. Some girls are available, some aren't."

"The girls on the street, for the most part, can't make it in the clubs."

"Hey, some of them look pretty young," Israel observes.

"I know, and I worry about that," I say. "This place is regulated, but I don't know how they enforce."

That has always been one of the main issues for me here, in La Coahuila. Some of the girls appear to be too young. True, the industry is semi-regulated. But there appears to be some cracks in the system. I have asked a few of them their age, and they always reply "nineteen", or "twenty-one", but I don't believe it sometimes. It's a damn shame, because some of them seem nice, and scared, and it bothers me. But what can I do? Invite one to live with me? Maybe. I've thought about it. Be the big hero, pull them out of the mess they are in, pay for their visa and move them over to San Diego. But it hasn't happened. I'm not in a financial position where I can afford to support another human being. And it's too bad. I would like to. And some of these girls deserve it.

Eduardo seems curious, so he asks us, "Can we check it out?"

"Check out what? Adelita's?"

"Yeah, I've never been there."

"Alright, we can go later. It's right around the corner."

We take care of our tab, pay our respects to the bartender, and walk out on the street. I'm always cordial to the bartenders; I know the score. If I frequent an establishment enough, a good rapport with the bartenders can go a long way. You will always be guaranteed great service. It's all politics, especially social politics. Social politics is a serious game in Tijuana. You have to know the right people.

We make our way down the narrow street and turn right, into 'La Coahuila.' You know it as soon as you are there.

As we walk by, some girls whistle, and some try to grab, or 'hook' you. One of them curls her finger and catches Israel on the sleeve as he walks by.

"Now I realize why they are called 'Hookers,' " he says.

"Yep. That's how they do it."

We walk down a little further, by a place called "Kentucky Fried Buches."

Israel looks up at the 'Kentucky Fried Buches' sign and inquires, "What are *buches?*"

Ricardo looks at him, "They're fried chicken necks. Greasy as hell, but if you're drunk they go down well."

"Yeah, I wouldn't eat them now. Wait until you're liquored up a bit, then you won't care if you're eating deep-fried chicken necks or not."

"Sounds good."

We laugh at the dilapidated 'Colonel' painted next to the sign and move on down.

"Ok, where to next?"

"There's this bar called the Zacazonapan. It's probably the craziest dive bar in TJ. No hookers, though, but plenty of anything else," I inform them.

"What's anything else?"

"Beer, liquor, drugs, whatever. You can score anything you want in the 'Zaca', and the cops ignore it."

"What do mean, ignore it?"

"Oh, they go in, but they don't bust anybody. I've seen guys do lines right on the bar. The bartender can hook you up. The cops go right in and just make sure nothing violent is happening. They ignore anything else."

"Only in Coahuila?" Israel asks.

"Yes."

"Where is this place at?"

"Oh, it's hard to find. It's just a small entrance leading to a basement."

"Let's go."

We walk back to "Kentucky Fried Buches", and the entrance to the Zacazonapan is right next door. It is an unmarked entrance leading down to stairs that will take you to a basement where the bar is located. You can walk past it five times and never find the entrance. You can't find it on your own; you will need a guide of sorts. We know where it is, so we make our way down to the basement. The Zacazonapan sells cahuamas only, unless you want something strong. The jukebox is good, and that is one of the keys to the Zaca. A place is not good unless the music is good. If the music is good, and the beer is cold, then it is an establishment I can 'frequent.' Those are pretty much the ingredients for success. Cold beer and good music. Plus the fact that you can score almost any type of drug without fear of reprisal adds to the ambiance. The Zaca is one of the reasons I come down to Tijuana.

This is one of the characteristics of Tijuana that adds to the flavor of the city: the Tolerance Zones. There is a Tolerance Zone for prostitution. Also, individual establishments can be Tolerance Zones unto themselves. For instance, the Zacazonapan is a Tolerance Zone. Drugs of any nature can be procured there, in full view of the police. The Municipal Police of Tijuana make frequent rounds of the Zacazonapan, but no corrective action is made. Patrons of the bar are free to consume any amount of beer or any type of drug with impunity. This is not the only "Tolerance' establishment in Tijuana. There is another vendor, along Calle Ocampo, that we refer to as "Oasis." "Oasis" sells a variety of items, most importantly beer and Clamato. Although they have tables inside, they also sell clama-cheves to go, on a counter on the street. Even in Tijuana, selling alcohol on the street is illegal, but you will often see Police officers themselves frequenting "Oasis", because it is the best clama-cheve you can find in the city. The Police, along with the citizens of Tijuana, value it, so they ignore, or 'Tolerate' the practice of selling alcohol on the street. This is a characteristic of Tijuana. Rule of Law does not exist here; rather, Rule of Law with exceptions, defined as tolerance, is the norm. It is this 'tolerance' that defines Tijuana and makes it exceptional. You won't find tolerance like this, so close to the United States, where nothing is tolerated outside of the law. This attitude defines the city, and it defines the people that inhabit the city. Everyone deserves their own Tolerance Zone.

We find the entrance to the Zacazonapan, and walk downstairs to the basement. People down here for the first time can get uncomfortable. Most of us have been here before, so it's old hat for us.

"This place is shady, to say the least."

"It's a good bar, though. And cheap."

"How long has it been here?"

"Good question. I don't know, but it's been here awhile. We can ask."

"No, no don't bother. I don't want to look stupid asking the bartender how long he's been here."

At the bar I'm sitting next to Adrian. Israel is in the bathroom, and Ricardo and Eduardo are at the jukebox. This is my opportunity.

"Adrian, so what the hell happened yesterday?"

Adrian stares at me for a second before answering.

"What happened is you left me hanging. I'm damn lucky I got out of there without going to prison."

"Hey, I didn't know what to do."

"And that's the problem. Don't invite me in on something and then not know what to do. The only way I got out of there is they caught somebody else over in the car lanes. They forgot about me, so I left."

"What did you do with the stuff?"

"I still have it. I stashed it in my house."

"Ok, give it to me later and I can unload it on Jake."

"No, how about you just give me Jake's number? I can unload it myself, thanks."

I think about this. Adrian could be potential competition, but I can't refuse. I almost got him thrown in jail.

The guy next to us at the bar appears to overhear our conversation, because he keeps looking over his shoulder. He is a typical Tijuana punk. He is wearing a white t-shirt with the sleeves cut off. The back of his shirt reads, "Negu Gorriak." He has a studded belt, and a pair of jeans that have been in use for a few years, with minimal washings in between. The dead giveaway to his social status, though, is his shoes. He is wearing green 'Doc' Martens. The 'Docs' are a type of boot, coming in different colors, that define the old punk rocker. His particular 'Docs' appear to be a few years old, but well polished. This guy doesn't take care of himself, or the rest of his clothes, but any good punk will take special care of his 'Docs'. They're important. I can tell the soles are wearing down, but the leather is still good. That is one of the defining characteristics of the 'Doc' Marten. The leather will outlast the sole itself, and sometimes might outlive the owner. Those shoes are so long-lasting, they could become family heirlooms, passed down from generation to generation.

However, he keeps looking over his shoulder, so I inquire, "Fermin Muguruza hasn't been in town in awhile. What's up with that?"

That seems to catch his attention. "What do you know about Fermin? I just heard you speaking English, and I thought it was weird in here."

"Yeah, I agree. It is weird in here. But what's 'normal' in the Zaca anyway?"

He nods his head, then goes back to his beer. My knowledge of Fermin Muguruza probably spared me a good beating, but that's how it goes down here. You better know what you're doing if you are going to walk into a bar like this, even with friends. I've been alone in here, but I think twice before I do that. I have to possess a real thirst if I want to walk in here alone. One bad move or moment of ignorance can cost you in a bar like the Zaca.

We have a few beers, which are cold, and put some more money in the jukebox. The Zacazonapan has a decent jukebox, and we make our selections. Since the Zaca is a punk bar, the jukebox has plenty of selections. Manu Chao is always a favorite in Tijuana, so we play a few of his songs. He always gets a good response from the citizens of Tijuana's underground when his music comes on. Anybody that frequents the Zacazonapan will instantly recognize Manu. A couple people actually applaud when they hear "Merry Blues" come on, a rarity in here. I know our choices are going to go over well. Tijuana is notoriously hard on musicians. A few years ago, ——— played a show at Plaza Monumental de Playas. At the time they were one of the most popular bands in Mexico, and are still world-famous. The band members decided to visit Adelita's afterwards, and they were instantly recognized. The manager of the brothel grabbed a microphone and asked them to sing a song, on stage. They refused. The crowd started booing, shouting

'Que se vaya!, Que se vaya!' and the band had to leave. Tijuana can turn on anybody in a heart-beat. I order another Cahuama when I feel a tap on my shoulder. Then I hear my name.

"Evan, damn it. I've been looking everywhere for you."

"Gerardo, what's up brother? My partner in crime. Take a seat, man. You've been looking for me?"

I'm surprised to see Gerardo down here. He rarely makes trips to this part of town. However, his brother, Gustavo, is a regular in Coahuila. Gerardo looks worried, so I get a sense of where this conversation is going to lead before he even gets started.

Gerardo waves off the bartender. "Hey, have you seen Gustavo? I got a call from him, and he might be in trouble. I can't find him, though."

I introduce Gerardo to the rest of the gang, but they have met before.

"Trouble? No, I haven't run into him. I just got down here, though. Everything ok.?"

"I don't know. If he's in trouble though, he's probably somewhere around here."

"No clue, but let's ask."

I ask the bartender, describing Gustavo, but the barkeep shakes his head. He's never seen him.

"He's probably in a club," Israel quips.

"I agree. Where does he usually go?" I ask Gerardo. "Adelita's, or Chicago's? Probably Adelita's."

"Yeah, knowing Gustavo he probably went into Adelita's. If he was too drunk though, they'll throw him out, especially if he doesn't have money."

"Did he have any money?" Adrian asks. Gustavo is typically broke, and always in between jobs.

"Maybe, unless his unemployment came in. When that happens, he usually blows the whole check down here."

"Yep, that sounds right."

"Can you guys help me look for him?"

"Who are we looking for?" Ricardo steps in and asks.

"The other Sanchez brother." I explain.

"Yeah, I need some help." Gerardo says.

Gerardo directs his request to the whole group. Everybody looks at me. I doubt the people I'm with will want to drop what they are doing to help out Gustavo. They hardly know him. This isn't the first time this has happened.

"Alright, hold on," I tell him. "Let us finish our beer and we'll head out."

"Did you check the police station here?" Israel asks him.

"No," Gerardo answers. "Wouldn't they take him to the 'La Ocho'?"

"If they picked him up anyplace else, yes, they would take him to 'La Ocho.' " I tell Gerardo. "But if they picked him up here, there is a small police station in La Coahuila."

"Can we check there?"

"Yeah, don't worry. If he's there, he's not going anywhere unless he can pay off the cops and the lawyer."

"How much do we need?" Gerardo inquires.

"We?" I ask. "Who's we?" Gerardo gives me a dirty look. "Just kidding. Relax, Israel and I have been thrown in the drunk-tank here before. Other than having to spend some cell time with transvestite hookers and drunks pissing on themselves, he should be fine."

70

Israel leans over to Gerardo, "Oh yeah, Evan and I had to spend a night in there one time. All you have to do is be respectful to the cops, and they'll leave you alone until you can make bail. Just don't mouth off."

"Yeah, they kicked the shit out of a guy in there for being disrespectful."

"No, they beat his ass for being a thief."

"I don't remember that," Adrian claims.

"Because you were in the other cell," I say. "They kept kicking him in the stomach, asking him if he was an *animal* or a *man*. He kept replying, 'man.' The cops wanted him to say 'animal.' He refused, so they kept kicking him. And every time they kicked him, they asked the same question: 'Humano ó Animal?' Then they would kick him again. He probably pissed blood for a week."

"I remember them beating on somebody, but I don't remember that. What I do remember was that little statue of the Vírgen de Guadalupe up in the corner of that room. The Vírgen was overlooking the cops beating on that guy."

"As soon as they let him back in the cell, he rolled this drunk old man who was passed out on the floor and took his pocket money. I told him, 'Hey, you just got your ass kicked for that.' He didn't care."

Israel and I forgot about Gerardo in our conversation, but I looked back and saw horror on his face.

"Relax, relax, he's fine. It's still early anyway. Nobody should be drunk right now."

"You never know."

"Alright, let's go."

Israel and I killed off our Cahuamas and we hit the street. Adrian, Ricardo, and Eddie stayed in the bar. The small police station was only a few stores down from where we were, but most people would miss it. It's extremely small. They have two holding tanks in the back, and a small office in the front. This Municipal police station just processes local trouble, and they mostly handle prostitutes, pimps and small-time hustlers who try to profit on the wayside in La Coahuila. Most of it is petty-theft and the like, but they do pull in the occasional drunk. In Coahuila, if you're drunk but have money, you are fine with the cops. Once you run out of money though, you're done. Israel and I got pulled in because a prostitute off the street accused Israel of grabbing her ass as he walked by. He denies this, but that's what the cops stuck with when they booked us. I was just happy they didn't beat us down. They certainly shook us down, taking cash off both of us.

"Hey," I look over at Israel, "do you still claim you didn't man-handle that girl?"

Israel looks at me for a second or two, then remembers, "No, I did not."

"Cost me fifty bucks."

"Are you still complaining about that?"

"Yes, I hope it was worth it."

"Worth every penny."

"I knew it! You bum."

Gerardo looks confused, "What are you guys talking about?"

"Ancient history. Let's go find Gustavo, before he gets his liver kicked in."

VII

Gustavo was nowhere to be found, either in the Police station or on the street.

"We're going to have to try Adelita's, or some of the fringe bars."

"That's no good for us," Israel says. "I'm not walking into one of these side-bars. You got to be fucking crazy."

"Let's try Adelita's first, then we'll figure it out from there."

"Alright."

"Where's Adelita's?"

"On Calle Coahuila."

"Coahuila, or Cahuila?"

"Well, it's spelled Coahuila. But anybody down here pronounces it 'La *Cahuila*.'"

"Why?"

"I don't know, but if you sound it out as Coahuila they'll know you're not local. Everybody down here pronounces it 'La *Cahuila*.' Don't forget the 'La.'"

Adelita's is right on Calle Coahuila, the heart of the Zona Norte. Adelita's is a large, spacious place. It has a very laid-back atmosphere. It's also the most infamous brothel in town. The women can be downright beautiful, and the traffic amongst foreigners is high. There's always a contingent of Asians, mostly Japanese, and a good number of Americans. The White and Asian clientele keeps the place respectable, and safe. A good amount of money is spent in that establishment, and I guarantee most of the Asian businessmen in suits are Maquiladora owners. In La Cahuila, this is as good as it gets. As you walk in, there is a large bar to the right, with a dance floor and tables behind and to the left. From time to time, there will be a pole dancer, but not always. The girls circle about, and that's where the action is. The men that patron Adelita's are not there to watch a strip show, but to pick up a woman, either by the hour or for the evening. The girls circle about, waiting for an invite or, if they get desperate enough, volunteer to sit next to a guy. Everything is low key and relaxed here. It's a different vibe than the rest of the Coahuila strip clubs. We walk in, and I make my way to the bar. This should make my intentions known that I'm not 'in the market' and I just want a beer. We scan the crowd.

"No sign of him."

"Unless he took a girl upstairs already."

"Maybe."

"This guy," Israel says, shaking his head.

"When did he call?" I ask. "Was he worried?"

"No, he left a message. Told me to pick him up. Said he was down in Tijuana, down here in Coahuila. He was definitely drunk."

"Alright, let me ask."

I ask a waiter, giving Gustavo's name and his description. The bartender points up. That means he's next door, upstairs with a woman. Then he leans over and and gives me the details on Gustavo's latest adventure here.

"He's here, Gerardo, just wait."

"That bastard. Damn it, it's barely nine o'clock!"

"Yeah, the bartender told me the cops already picked him up. He made bail, then came back."

"What, he was already in the tank?"

"Yeah, I guess he's been down here all day."

"Oh, my god," Gerardo says. "Already in and out of the tank, and upstairs with a woman. It's barely nine o'clock!"

"You just said that."

"Why did he call?"

"He probably wanted a ride back, that's all."

We all laugh. Gustavo is probably broke by now. He can blow through his whole paycheck in a few hours down here. That happens to many gentlemen who discover the pleasures and the traps of La Coahuila.

"Well, at least he's not in trouble."

"Yeah, and I want to keep it that way."

"If anybody sees me here, you better vouch for me," I inform Israel and Gerardo.

"Don't worry, we're your alibi. Might as well enjoy while you're here Evan, because you have an ironclad excuse."

"Yeah, this is like a free ride. Gaby can't get mad at you for being down here now. You're helping out a friend," Israel says.

"True."

We spend another hour or so at the bar inside Adelita's. It's a decent crowd tonight, and no problems, but it is still early. You don't want to be in this place after three in morning, because that's when the trouble will come. Kids with guns and too much to drink enter the scene, and that's usually my curtain call. Once we see the crowd shift, it's our turn to leave. Too bad, because it was turning into a good night. It was somber for the first half hour, but then Gustavo finally decided to show his face and he was glad to see us. He had his ride home. He spent all of his money on bail and his woman, so we end up buying him beers. I don't mind tonight. I never mind on a night like this. I buy a round of beers. Then Israel signals the bartender and pays for another. I buy another round, then Gerardo chips in and pays for a fourth round of beers. The night turned cool, with a nice breeze coming in from the door. The breeze felt different, like a storm brewing just off the coast. I believe I can feel it; maybe it will be the last one of the season. You get that human sixth sense for a storm. Inside, you can feel it. There's something in the atmosphere; you can't identify it, but it is there, and you know it is coming. The beers start to hit me, finally, and I feel myself a bit off-balanced. Best to excuse myself, I say. I bid my farewell, despite the protests, and make my way onto the street, alone.

* * * *

I abandon everybody. I feel like being alone. I don't have the energy anymore to continue drinking. I want to take a walk. I need to sober up a bit. A walk is always an interesting experience in Tijuana, especially at one in the morning. From La Coahuila, I walk down Calle Primera, then I turn on Avenida Niños Heroes. I pass the La Cathedral, the central church in Tijuana. The Cathedral is enormous; the two bell-towers in front strut up from the sidewalk. There are spotlights on the towers, giving it a spectral glow. They look imposing at night. I walk by, but the large wooden doors are closed. I push on them, to see if they will open. They don't. They must weigh half a ton each. The doors are large, part of the largest church in Tijuana. It is in the middle of everything. It's proximity to La Coahuila is suspect. I wonder about that—Tijuana's main Cathedral, next to La Coahuila. I walk back towards Calle Constitución, then stroll all the way down the street. I pass boarded up shops, small parking garages, and open bars. Avenida Constitución runs parallel to Avenida Revolución. I pass the *Cine Bujazan*, the old theatre of Tijuana. The theater isn't active anymore; it partially burned down in nineteen ninety-four. The façade is still up. Alan Zamora, drummer for a big punk band here in Tijuana, wants to turn it into a music venue. It has all the characteristics of a good venue; great acoustics, plenty of space, and good location; right in the heart of Centro de Tijuana. I've been inside, once. The roof burned down, but the walls are all intact. The lobby was spared most of the destruction. A lot of the old moldings still exist inside the lobby. It is very ornate, with an antique feel to it. As you walk to the back, the main amphitheater of the *Bujazan* is still up, but in ruins. Everything is open-air, because of the roof. It has a postapocalyptic quality to it, like a survivor from a nuclear holocaust. It's a great place for a show. I walk past it, over to the police station on Calle Ocho. I turn the corner and walk down the road leading to the Jai Alai Palace.

The old Jai Alai Palace is a cultural landmark in Tijuana. It's a large structure, designed to host the ancient Basque sport of Jai Alai. They haven't hosted a Jai Alai tournament since the early nineties. The large Jai Alai sign is still there, lit up in the night. The sign is red, and it reads, "Jai Alai." There is no Jai Alai in Tijuana any more. Now, it is a venue for concerts and anything else it can host. I have seen plenty of good shows there. Big Reggae festivals are held there every year. Cultura Profetica, Gondwana, Los Cafres, the best Reggae and Jazz from Latin America have all played there. In front is a large sculpture of the planet earth, with a Jai Alai player standing on top of it. The player is holding a *xistera*, the standard banana-shaped racquet they use. The planet has a spot-light underneath it, lighting it up at night. The planet has an ethereal glow, especially with the Jai Alai palace as a backdrop. The Jai Alai player is holding his *xistera* like a trophy. It is well lit in the night. I sit down next to the Jai Alai player and I light a cigarette. I hear music behind me. The music is coming from Las Pulgas, the prototypical Tijuana Disco. You can hear the music of Las Pulgas from blocks around, reverberating in alleyways and up and down La Revu. I have been to Las Pulgas before. It is called "Las Pulgas" because it used to be a flea market, before they transformed it. It had another name when it first opened, but people kept referring to it as "Las Pulgas", which means "The Fleas." The name stuck. One of the best discothèques in Tijuana is named "The Fleas." It is one of the largest Discos in Tijuana, with multiple dance floors blaring different types of Mexican folk music. They have different rooms, with slightly different folk music between them. They all have one design: to make people dance. The beer is cheap, and sold by the bucket. The dance floors are always crowded. All the social status of Tijuana will be found there. Plenty of single women, in groups, looking for men who will buy the table a bucket of beer and ask them to dance. Las Pulgas is across the street from the Jai Alai. At this time of night, there are plenty of drunks reeling through the exit, and there a few cops waiting outside to hassle them. It's shake-down time for the police officers of Tijuana. Time for the cops to make some money, and their victims are unwitting drunks stumbling out of the club. The drunks will always pay up. The cops have pushed a couple of them up against the wall, asking them questions and checking their pockets. I smoke my cigarette and watch the whole operation from across the street as the police officers of Tijuana make their breakfast money. When I finish my cigarette, I stand up and walk across the street. I cruise by the Chiki Jai, a small Basque restaurant. It is quiet and small, and I enjoy eating there. It is right on the corner, smartly colored. The food is traditional Basque, for the most part. It is small, but well lit at night. During the day, they open all the wooden windows, and the breeze is nice in there. As Hemingway said, it is a clean, well lit place. The Paella is outstanding. The 'Chiki Jai' title is a Basque title, and it opened up to complement the Jai Alai Palace in the nineteen–forties. The Chiki-Jai has been open since 1944, in the middle of World War II. In those times, you could enjoy the Basque sport of Jai Alai and then walk over to the Chiki-Jai and enjoy a nice Basque meal. You can still enjoy the meal, but the sport has long since disappeared.

I continue, and I walk past Calle Sexta. La Sexta holds the bar 'Dandy's del Sur', a beautiful dive bar. It has a twenty–four hour liquor license, and it is famous amongst the locals. If you need a drink at eight in the morning, it is open and ready to serve. I make my way over there. I walk inside, past the gaudy painting of a half-naked woman, and take a seat at the bar. A woman serves me a Bohemia. The beer is cold, and good. I will have another. I can smoke right on the bar, so I order a pack of cigarettes. The woman brings me an ashtray. The ashtray is a large clam shell. I dump my ashes in the clam shell and take my time smoking my cigarette, because I can. It feels calming to smoke and drink at the same time, at a bar, with a clam shell as an ash-tray. I don't have to go outside to smoke, as I do in the United States. I patron Dandy's del Sur frequently. The bar is dark, but the seats have nice cushions. Everybody is re-laxed inside. There are always a few people inside, whatev-er the hour. Dandy's is busiest between the hours of three to five o'clock in the morning. That's when all the young people go, after the other bars and clubs have closed down for the night. Nortec, a band, wrote a song about it a few years ago. The bar has been famous since. Before the song, it was the bar for the taxi drivers, bartenders, musicians, waiters and waitresses; the working class of Tijuana. After the song, it became trendy, so you see a host of people there. I miss the old clientele, but the new people are fine. There are never any problems in Dandy's del Sur. I enjoy my beer and my smoke. Maldita Vecindad plays in the background. "Any good juke box in Tijuana must have them," I think to myself. Dandy's is a true dive bar, but a dive bar you can take a date to. It is not clean, but clean enough. Gaby doesn't mind coming here. She won't request it, but if I want to come she won't complain. She will always run into a friend here, which is why she doesn't mind. If her friends visit here, then it must be alright with her. The people of Tijuana all come here. It is a Tijuana dive bar. I finish my beer and pay my tab. I have an option: I can pay in pesos or dollars. This time, I decide to pay in dollars. You just have to make sure they are exchanging you at the current rate. Right now, it's about twelve–to–one pesos to dollars. It's a bit safer to pay in pesos if you can't work out the math. This is another characteristic to Tijuana; both currencies are readily accepted. After I do the math and pay the tab, I walk outside. I look at the neon light designating the bar, "Dandy's del Sur." The neon light is bright against the night. Underneath, it reads "Cantina." The lights make the Cantina welcoming. I always feel good when I walk into Dandy's del Sur.

I walk over to Avenida Revolución, the bawdy heart of Tijuana. All the touristy clubs are located here. All the stereotypical Tijuana night clubs light up the Avenue. The lights are on. I wonder about that. As I walk past discothèques and the employees paid to lure people in, I wonder about the lights. A guy cat-calls me from across the street, trying to lure me into a strip club. Another guy grabs my shirt, trying to pull me in to his dance-club. Avenida Revolución is always lit up. I'm reminded of some song lyrics I'm particularly fond of, "Donde habrá la luz de la ciudad, capacidad iluminar tus sombras." I wonder about that. Where are the lights of the city, with the ability to shine light on my shadows? I don't know if they are here, in Tijuana. Tijuana's lights are different than the rest of the world, and I know this. Can I find a light here? I don't know if Tijuana has that light. It certainly tries.

I walk past all the night clubs and I arrive at a small hotel called "Hotel Nelson." It is the oldest hotel in Tijuana. The people of Tijuana use it as a landmark. People from Tijuana don't navigate with street-signs, as they do in the U.S. They navigate by landmarks. The Hotel Nelson is one of the landmarks. It also has a nice bar underneath. The Hotel Nelson is right in the middle of the action. It is where Avenida Revolución and Calle Primera meet. At that intersection is where the musicians make their contacts and find their gigs for the night. I sit at the outdoor café of the Hotel Nelson and have another beer. I watch the musicians as they connect with their clients. All the musicians are still there. Every type of music you can play in Mexico. The Trio can play Boleros, which is Romantic music. 'Románticas' in Spanish. The Norteños can also play Banda, if the band is large enough. You will rarely find a complete 'Banda' on the street because their prices are the most expensive. They all stand on the corner of Calle Primera and Revolución, competing for customers. This is why the best prices can be found here. Their methods on the curb to catch their clients are not much different than the women on the street. Their costumes are flamboyant; they are designed to attract attention. They are also looking for clients who pay in cash. They can pull in hundreds of dollars a night. A good Mariachi costume can cost hundreds of dollars. The boots on some of the good Norteño bands can cost that much, as well. You can see the snakeskin boots, glistening in the night. The Mariachi outfits are shiny, with brass and silver buckles everywhere. Their uniforms clink and rattle as they walk by. Rancheros and Trios wear expensive silk shirts, with elaborate designs on them. One of the musicians, part of a Trio, has brought his instrument out. The guitar player strums out some chords to passing cars, hoping to attract some attention. They stand on the street, like cab-callers, and clients drive by and negotiate curb-side. If a deal is made, the lead musician will whistle to the rest of his band, they will load up in a van that was waiting for them, and they will follow their client to his or her destination. This is how you secure a good Mariachi in Tijuana. Negotiation by curb-side. You can request specific songs. You can find out how many pieces their band holds. Everything is negotiable. There are dozens of bands tonight, looking for their meal money. I imagine they moonlight as musicians. They probably work by day, then suit up in whatever outfits they have, hit the street about eight in the evening, and wait for their gig to show up. It's not a bad way to supplement the income, and they pull in decent money. A good Mariachi can pull in over two hundred dollars an hour. The size of the Mariachi band will determine the price.

I always wonder about that. What's the difference, really, between the musicians and the women on the street? They both work off of the street. They both offer a service. The both dress to attract attention. On the other hand, one industry is acceptable to society, the other is not. This may have to do with gender; the most noticeable difference is the separation of gender; the musicians are all male, the prostitutes are mostly female. Does it have any role in how their prospective industries are viewed? Probably.

I leave the café at the Hotel Nelson, and I walk up to a taco stand, still open. It is a beacon of life when everything is closing down in the early morning. The taco stand is lit up, and steam is rising from the grill. A prostitute, one of the young women of the street, is standing next to it. I wave her over. I ask her if she is hungry, and she replies that she is. I ask her name. She is surprised at this. Most men that frequent La Coahuila don't care about names.

"Marisol," she replies.

"Mucho gusto," I reply. I offer my hand to her. She looks at it, and then shakes my hand. She gives me a smile.

"¿Habla Inglés?" I ask her.

"Yes, I speak a little."

"Good."

"Do you want anything to eat?" I ask. "My treat."

She shakes her head, but I get the feeling she must be hungry. She's probably been working all night.

"Are you sure?" I look over at the taquero. "Dos tacos, para la Señorita."

He serves them up to her.

"Where are you from? ¿De dónde eres?"

She hesitates for a second, not sure whether to answer my question.

"Acapulco."

"Acapulco? Really? Which do you prefer? Tijuana, or Acapulco?" I ask her in Spanish.

"Acapulco. But there is work in Tijuana, so I am here."

"¿Cuanto años tienes?"

"Twenty-one."

"Are you sure?" I smile at her.

"Yes, I am sure."

I'm not sure. I doubt it. They always say 'twenty-one.' Don't believe it. It's probably closer to seventeen.

"How long have you been here, in Tijuana?"

"Tres meses."

"When do you go back to Acapulco?"

"No sé. I do not know. When I get enough money."

"Money for what?"

She looks at me. One too many questions. I drop it. I enjoy the rest of my taco. She has already finished her meal. Then she leans over to me.

"These tacos are no good."

The taquero looks over at her, but he laughs.

"¿Por qué no?" he asks.

"Tacos dorados."

"What's wrong with fried tacos?" I ask.

She glances back at me, "You shouldn't fry tacos. That's very bad."

The taquero responds, "But that's what everybody likes."

"It's bad for you," she tells me.

"How do you know?" I ask, intrigued.

"I went to school to cook. It's bad to make tortillas this way."

"Is it really?" I reply, "well, anything fried is bad for you."

She smiles, finally. "Yes, very bad for you. They shouldn't make tortillas this way."

"How do you make them?"

"From corn. That's the best way."

"Your school taught you this?"

"Yes."

"So, why work here then?"

"I want to run taco stand too, back in Acapulco. But bigger than this. I want to open one. I need the money."

"Nice. How long was the school? In the U.S., it's called 'culinary' school."

She doesn't understand the word 'culinary,' so I describe it in Spanish. I ask her how many years she attended school in Acapulco to learn how to cook.

"Un año. One year."

"And you're going to open a place when you get back?"

"I want to. But the money isn't good like I thought it was. It's ok., but I thought it was going to be better."

Her English is excellent.

"Where did you learn your English?"

"In school."

"How did you get here?"

She doesn't answer, and the taquero shakes his head at me. Wrong question, down here. I change tactics, back to what works.

"What else do you cook?"

"Mexican, but traditional. Mexican food can be healthy, but you have to cook it right."

Maybe she is over eighteen, but just barely.

"Is all of your family in Acapulco? Or is anybody here?"

"All of them in Acapulco. I came here with a friend."

"Do you like working here?"

She shrugs her shoulders. It's a reality. Desire has nothing to do with it. She needs money to get started, and the money is here. There aren't a lot of options in most parts of Mexico. She is young, and seems to be a nice person. It's not right that she has to make a living on her back, but it's a reality for her down here. Sacrifice now, respectable tomorrow.

"Where do you live?"

"Outside Tijuana, over by Tecate. The place is called 'Maclovio Rojas.' "

I recognize that name. Maclovio Rojas has been in the newspapers here in Tijuana. The 'Mayor' of Maclovio Rojas, a woman by the name of Hortensia Mendoza, is always causing some sort of commotion. Her situation is unique.

"The female-run community?"

"Yes, that's the one," she replies.

"The Zapatista one?"

"Yes."

For some bizarre reason, Maclovio Rojas has a strange connection to the Zapatista movement in Chiapas. I remember because Maclovio Rojas attempted to open its own school, autonomous of the State education system. The only other one to exist was in Chiapas. Hortensia herself is a bit of a rabble-rouser. She enjoys stirring the pot. It's good publicity for her community, if nothing else. Maclovio Rojas has been a thorn in the side of the Mexican State government for years now, compounded by the fact that the community was founded and is run by women. Another Tijuana miracle, to be sure. However, there is some wisdom in a female run community.

"Is Hortensia still there?"

"Yes, she just got out of jail. They never keep her for a long time."

"What did she do this time?"

"Refused to pay taxes, or some fee."

"Good for her."

"Well, she went to jail. They harass her in there."

"They probably do."

I order her one more taco. The taquero waves my dollar bill away. He won't take my money for her food. I make sure I leave him a good tip. She seems happy by this, and she seems to finally open up. She finally looks me in the eyes when she speaks to me. She is small, with dark eyes and dark hair. She is thin, but built in the right places. She is not beautiful by most standards, but she is attractive enough. I tell her she should try to get into a club. Maybe just dance, because you can make money that way, too. She tells me they won't let her in. She's not tall enough, she is too dark, and the foreigners wouldn't like her. I tell her that is not true, and she should keep trying. The taquero agrees. By her speech, I can tell she is intelligent. She speaks quickly, and with authority, especially when it comes to food. She is twenty years old and she is responsible for people. She has a head on her shoulders. She tells me she has a small family, and they don't have a lot of money. I ask her about crossing up to the United States, and she replies that she would rather live in Acapulco. I tell her I could help her cross; I know a few honest people that can help her cross. They wouldn't take her money and run. She says no thanks. She has family that she wants to be with and help support in Acapulco. She is twenty years old and is responsible for a family. I ask her what part of the street she works. She points to a small hotel on the corner of Constitución and Calle Coahuila. I tell her I will look out for her in the future. I give her a twenty dollar bill, 'for the food stand,' then I wave goodbye.

VIII

I walk back over to the Zacazonapan. Eddie, Ricardo, and Adrian should be long gone by now. Only it and Dandy's del Sur will be open for patrons at this time of night. Yesterday afternoon I had agreed to meet Gaby for breakfast over at the Espadaña, located in the Zona Rio. It's definitely Gaby's scene. I told Gaby we would meet there at nine o'clock this morning. There's no use for me to go to sleep now. I might as well have a few drinks, then head over to the Espadaña afterwards.

I walk down to the basement where the Zacazonapan is located. I order a drink, and I ask the bartender what time it is. He replies, "seis de la mañana." "Bien, gracias." I have enough time for a couple drinks before I will have to catch a cab down to the restaurant. I also ask him when my compatriots left the bar, and he responds about an hour ago. The beer leaves a bitter taste in my mouth. I sobered up while on my extended walk through Centro de Tijuana.

Good. I don't want to arrive drunk at nine in the morning for my breakfast with Gaby. It wouldn't leave a good impression. Gaby is known to forget about her dates, but she never misses a breakfast at La Espadaña. It is an excellent place for breakfast. She wants to arrive early, because it can get crowded. Mexicans eat breakfast much later than Americans. Peak breakfast hour there is about ten to eleven in the morning.

I drink a few beers, put some money in the juke box, and wait out the morning. The bartender places a bowl of *chicharones* onto to the bar. We both eat them while listening to the music. I inform him that I will buy him a beer if he drinks it with me. The bartender is agreeable. He pulls a cahuama out of the fridge underneath the bar and cracks it open. We share the *chicharones* and drink our beer. He asks me what I'm up to at this hour and I inform him that I have a breakfast date later this morning. He laughs at this and asks me if the girl is worth it. I reply that she is. He advises me not to drink too much. I agree, but I inform him that once you start on a binge like this, it's hard to stop. He nods his head.

I know the sun must be coming up by now. I saw the early morning glow as I walked in earlier. I could also feel the air pressure on my lips and in my nose. I can tell it I going to be a hot day. It's going to be a hot summer, so they say. After I finish my last beer I bid goodbye to the bartender and walk back up the stairs and onto the street. The daylight hits my eyes and I am temporarily blinded. The light hurts my eyes. That always happens when you are indoors when the sun comes up. It takes a minute to adjust. Spending daybreak in the dungeon of the Zacazonapan does this to me. It's not the most romantic way to spend a sunrise, but it is the Tijuana way. I walk over to Calle Primera and hail a cab. There are a few cabs waiting in the morning, but they seem surprised to see me there. There are three cab-drivers huddled around one of the taxis and their breakfast is spread out over the hood. The cabs are lined up along the street. One of them finishes his meal and rushes up to escort me to his car. The best way to procure a cab in Tijuana is to negotiate the price of the fare in advance; otherwise they will give you the extended tour of Tijuana and charge you twice the amount they should. The cab-driver opens the door for me and questions me on my destination. I give him instructions on how to get to the restaurant. The cab-driver seem annoyed by this, and he tells me that he knows how to get there. I apologize but I instruct him that I want to get there in under an hour. He takes me through Avenida Revolución, down Calle Sexta, and all the way through the Paseo de los Héroes. The cab takes me through the gloriettas of Paseo de los Héroes. There is heavy traffic this morning, and the cabbie has a hard time merging in and out of the flow of the glorietta. As we drive I look up and take note of all the monuments in the middle of the gloriettas. All traffic must go around the monuments, like a horizontal Ferris Wheel. We pass the Benito Juarez sculpture, then drive around Padre Kino statue. Then we come up to the glorietta that possesses the Abraham Lincoln monument. Lincoln is there, in his suit and top-hat, holding a broken chain. I suppose the broken chain represents slavery. The monument is very majestic. It is odd to see an American President represented by monument in Tijuana, but there it is. Lincoln abolished slavery. Lincoln was right about many things. What the monument should really represent is the fact that Lincoln, a United States Representative, was one of the few who opposed the Mexican-American War. He was vocal against us declaring war on Mexico with the sole purpose of acquiring territory. He declared it opportunistic. We were taking advantage of a neighbor in a compromised position. It was a rare moment of clarity and truth emanating from a politician. A true rarity. He was calculating, like all politicians, but in that instance I see a grain of honesty. He claimed it was wrong, and he was right. That, more than the chain, should be up in the monument.

We circle Lincoln's monument, then make our way up to Boulevard Sánchez-Taboada, where the best restaurants of the Zona Rio are located. The driver come up to La Diferencia and tries to stop, but I inform him he needs to drive down to the next restaurant. He tells me La Diferencia is a better restaurant than La Espadaña. I agree with him, but only regarding dinner. For breakfast I prefer La Espadaña. Dinner is better served at La Diferencia.

We stop, I pay my fare and leave a tip, and I walk into La Espadaña. I reserve a table. It is still a bit early, so I sit down right away, waiting for Gaby. She will probably be late, knowing I will be on time and waiting for her with a table. I order a Michelada. I am hungry, but I will wait for Gaby. She will consider it the height of rudeness if I eat now, not waiting for her. It's best to avoid that. I drink my Michelada and watch the families enjoying their meal. La Espadaña is a large restaurant, decorated with a Spanish motif and tables crowded throughout. Conversations echo through the restaurant, so I can't follow anything specific.

There are large and small families mixed in with young couples enjoying their breakfast. La Espadaña manages to be both chic and family-oriented at the same time.

Finally, Gaby walks up. She is wearing tight jeans, boots, and a blouse. The jeans highlight all of her curves. Everything she wears is always tight on her; her clothes never leave anything to the imagination. She always wears expensive, designer jeans. It's one of the few items I consider a good investment; a good pair of jeans can go a long way. They can be casual, or formal. They can last years. Mexican women were made to wear tight jeans. They are a perfect fit. It requires a certain physique to pull off tight jeans, and most Mexican women have it. Gaby is one of those women. She sits down without greeting me.

"What time did you get here?" she asks.

"Oh, about a half-hour ago."

"Are you ok.? You look a mess."

"Thanks."

"What happened? Don't tell me you were up all night."

"I wasn't." I lied. "I got up late and didn't have time to get ready."

"That's a bad excuse."

"It's the one I have."

She looks at me. She knows I'm lying, but leaves it at that.

"What are you going to order? I see you already ordered your drink."

"Yeah, I know. I needed a pick-me-up. I think I'll order *chilaquiles rojos.*"

"I agree. *Chilaquiles rojos.* That's the reason I come."

"You can't go wrong with them."

We both look around the restaurant. La Espadaña is always busy in the morning. Families and couples fill the tables around us. Waiters and waitresses fly around the restaurant, taking and filling orders as fast as possible. Steam from the coffee pots rise up to the ceiling. A waitress walks over to us with her steaming pewter coffee pot. Gaby orders a cup of *café de la olla con canela*. She asks if I want one, but I reply that it is too sweet for me. My Michelada will suffice. "If I want coffee, I'll take it black," I inform her. Gaby replies that this is the best cup of coffee you can find. She scans the restaurant again.

"I love this restaurant."

"I know you do. That's why we come. Are Adrian and Sonia coming?"

"Sonia is. Maybe Hector. Adrian, I don't know. Sonia didn't mention anything about him. But you probably know more about that than me."

"I don't think Adrian is going to make it."

She looks at me. My mind works back a few hours to Adrian's condition when I left the bar. I doubt he'll be here. I'm not offering more than that. I change the subject.

"So, are we going to the Palenque this year, or what?"

"Oh? Yes! That's what I wanted to talk to you about. I think Hector is going to get tickets for us."

"Well, we'll see him right now," I tell her. "We can ask him. I want to go."

"Yes, me too. It's been a couple years. I've been wanting to go."

"Who do you want to see?"

"Probably Vicente. Valentin Elizalde is also going to be there. So is Joan Sebastian. Maybe El Buki. But I want to see 'Chente'."

"Yeah, he's getting old. He probably doesn't have many Palenques left in him."

"His shows are always the best. His act is designed for the Palenque."

"We'll see what Hector says."

"They should be here any minute."

Sonia and Hector Tellez arrive right before our food does. They are brother and sister, and look alike. You can tell they are siblings straight off. They have the same sad Moorish eyes. Gaby will probably want to wait to eat with them, but after my night I'm starving. Gaby greets them, then walks over to another table to greet a few friends that walked in earlier. Gaby stays over at their table. Sonia looks like she has something on her mind. I know what it is about.

"Evan, have you seen Adrian?" Sonia asks me. "You were out with him last night, no?"

"Yes, but he crossed the border," I reply between mouthfuls. "We got separated. He's probably sleeping right now."

"Yeah, probably."

"Why aren't you crashed out?" Hector asks.

"Oh, I'm fine. One night can't knock me out."

"Good man, Evan, good man."

Sonia shakes her head. "Don't encourage him, Hector. Especially since they didn't invite us."

"You were invited. Sonia, you're always invited. It's not my fault that it turned into a guy's night out. Adrian should have invited you."

"True."

"If I had invited you, though...would you have gone?"

"Yes. I don't care where I drink."

Sonia was right. She can be one of the guys if she wants to. Gaby doesn't have that quality, but Sonia does. I respect her for it.

"Sonia, have you been to the Zacazonapan before?"

"Yes, once or twice," she tells me. "I don't really like it. But I do like Dandy's. You know that bar because of me. I put it on the map."

It's true. Sonia always finds the best bars and restaurants first. Her, and Hector. They recommended 'Dandy's' to me in the first place. Sonia isn't afraid to walk into a place. Gaby will always wait for Sonia. If Sonia gives it her approval, then Gaby will go.

"Damn, I think I picked the wrong cousin. Sonia, you and I would have had a great time together. We could go all through Tijuana, sampling all the bars and restaurants first."

"Ha! Yeah, I know," Sonia tells me, "too bad we're stuck with a couple of stiffs."

"Be careful, here comes one of those stiffs right now."

Gaby walks back to our table, greets Sonia and Hector with a kiss on the cheek, and sits down.

"Your food is getting cold."

"I know, but a couple friends from school are over there. I had to say 'hi.' It would be rude not to."

"Here's Gaby, always running into friends," Sonia says. "Don't you know you're making Evan here jealous?" Sonia winks at me. Hector laughs, then orders a Michelada.

Hector looks at my Michelada, "See, a true compatriot. I respect a man that can drink a beer at nine in the morning."

I raise my glass to him, "Hector, you're a good guy. So what's going on with the Palenque tickets?"

"Oh, yes! Hector, were counting on you!" Gaby was very excited about this concert.

"Who do you want to see?" Hector asks them.

"Vicente," say Sonia and Gaby together.

"Really? There's a few good shows this year."

"Yeah, there are. I wouldn't mind seeing Joan Sebastian," I say. "Especially if he does the show on horse-back."

"I agree. Joan Sebastian puts on a good show at the Palenque, especially if he sings on horse-back. I would want to see that."

"Joan Sebastian isn't bad, but Chente is the main event," Sonia informs us.

"Definitely Chente," Gaby gets in.

"Alright, I should be able to get tickets easy enough. I think they are already on sale."

"What are you waiting for?"

"Don't worry; he's playing for two nights. The tickets for the 16th of September will be the difficult ones to find. But I have my sources." He winks and takes a long drink of his Michelada.

"We will have a good time."

"Always. Who's coming with us?" Hector looks at Sonia. All social events go through her as well as Hector.

"Adrian, obviously," Sonia says. "Let's invite Israel and Susana as well."

"Really? Suzie?" I ask. "Can't we invite Israel by himself?"

"No, we can't do that," Gaby informs me. "We'll just invite them both. Susana can always duck out of it. I'm sure she will. I don't think she can be out all night like that."

"What, her parents?"

"How old is she?"

"Oh, she has to be at least twenty-four," Gaby answers. "Israel is her first boyfriend, though. I don't think they trust him yet."

"If they knew the truth, they wouldn't have anything to worry about." I say.

"Evan, don't be like that. He's your friend."

"I know he's my friend. They just don't have anything to worry about. And yes, definitely, invite them both. I don't think she will come."

"Ok., who else?"

"Ricardo?" I ask.

Hector replies at this one, "He's my brother, but I don't think that's the best idea. I don't think he can make it until four in the morning."

"I'll keep an eye on —"

"—No you won't, Evan" Gaby cuts in. "You'll be drinking yourself. I don't want to babysit anybody there. It's too much trouble."

Sonia thinks about it, then says "Yeah, we can invite my brother. If we're all there, he can't get into that much trouble. Just make sure he's not drinking hard liquor."

"That's going to be hard to do."

"I'll tell him to stick to beer. It's only when he gets into to heavy stuff that the trouble starts."

"Alright. And Eduardo?" I ask.

"Oh, definitely, if he's down here," Hector replies.

We all look at each other.

"It's settled, then?"

"Yes, the Palenque, for Día de la Independencia."

"Hector, make it happen."

We sit there for two hours, going over our previous Palenque experiences. Hector is in fine form, as is Sonia. I believe that Hector and Sonia are Gaby's two favorite people, so she's always agreeable when we are with them. They bring out the best in her. Gaby and Sonia are the same age, so they grew up together. They can chat for hours straight. You rarely see friends like that among women. I get along with Sonia. She has an easy social grace, like Gaby, but minus the character defects. Sonia is rather plain looking, but she has a way about her that is attractive enough. When you have a conversation with her, you know she understands. The eyes are the mark of intelligence; some people have it and some people don't. You can look somebody in the eye and know exactly who you are dealing with. Sonia can control a conversation, but you never feel inferior by it. We talk about going down to Ensenada, visiting the Valle de Guadalupe. We hope that the bullfighting season will be a good one. Hector informs us that the big weekend for Bullfights is coming up, and that we shouldn't miss it. We reply that we won't. We talk about going to the Hotel La Fonda, on the beach just south of Rosarito. The conversation is pleasant and we debate about our list of things to do over the next few months. We make many good plans. We enjoy our breakfast together, making our plans for the summer.

IX

Summertime in Tijuana is unique; a blend of the cosmopolitan and the curious. It is a mingling of the classes. What defines the city of Tijuana is the unusual social dynamic of necessity. The classes are thrown together here, not out of design but out of a bizarre set of circumstances. Some people are here because they want to be. Many denizens are here because they have to be. It is this unusual social fabric that defines the city. Everybody has to accommodate one another. Nowhere is this more evident than the Bullfights in Tijuana. The elite, bourgeois, and the rabble all make their presence known. It is a social event as it is anything else. The Aficionado element is there, but so is the social element. The reason is simple: ticket prices, to fit any economic or social status. You can purchase a "Palco", which is a box on the floor, for two hundred dollars. The Palcos have a viewing area just below the Barrera. Above the Palcos a ticket in Barrera will run you about eighty dollars. For the elite in Tijuana, these are reasonable prices. As you move up the bullring, the prices plummet. Preferente tickets run around thirty dollars. These are the tickets I normally buy. Above the Preferente is the General Admission. The "General Admission," or open seating, can run you ten dollars. For most of the citizenry of Tijuana, this is acceptable, either to take the family for an afternoon or go with your friends to turn it into a drinking competition. The scene created in Tijuana is similar in respects to the original "Old Globe" theatre that English playwright, William Shakespeare, made so famous. There is a seat for every social class, and a spectacle as well. Shakespeare's plays are famous for having jokes inserted in them for every caliber of person that attended his plays. Often times, the classes were ignorant of the others' jokes. The dynamic of a Tijuana Bullfight can fit that profile. The elite are there to see and be seen. The Corrida itself doesn't interest them. It is an event, a social event where their presence will identify and establish themselves. The Bourgeois are the Aficionada. They pay attention. The 'Aficion' is concerned with the integrity of the Bullfight in Tijuana. They uphold the standards. The 'Pueblo' is there to drink and carry on. As the corrida continues, their attention wanes as they consume alcohol. However, if you are there to party, the General Admission is the place to be. Most of the drunks will be found there. As you make your way up the stands, you make your way down the social ladder of Tijuana.

It was Friday afternoon and I had agreed to meet Israel and Susana at one of the tents in front of "El Toreo." They arrived before me, grabbed a table, and each had a glass of water in front of them.

"Suzie, have you been to a Bullfight before?" I ask her.

"Hmn. Maybe."

"How do you figure, 'Maybe?' Either you've been to a Bullfight or you haven't."

Susana just nods her head and mumbles to herself.

"Yes, she's been to a few corridas with her family," Israel says.

Eighty percent of the time, Israel has to answer her questions for her. She is just Israel's type: Docile and a-sexual. Mentally, I would put her around twelve years old.

"So, what are we going to do?"

"Let's eat here at the bullring. They should have the food stands up by now."

I disagree with that. On an afternoon such as this, good mariscos can go a long way. I don't desire hot food right now; I want something refreshing. I suggest something else.

"No, let's grab food at 'Mariscos Toreo.' I haven't been there in a while."

"I agree," Israel informs me. "It's hot enough outside that I can eat ceviche."

"Exactly. It has to be hot to eat ceviche right. You can't eat ceviche on a cold day."

"Tostadas *de ceviche de camarón* sound good to me. Along with a michelada."

"Of course, of course. Who eats ceviche without a beer? Nobody."

"Where is this place?" Susana asks.

"Right across the street, on Agua Caliente. It's right on the corner."

"Yeah, Hector will probably be there already. That's his pre-game spot."

"He always eats there before a corrida."

Mariscos "El Toreo" is a bit of a tradition on Boulevard Agua Caliente. A large U-shaped bar dominates the place, and they serve up ceviche and *aguachile* in large *molcajetes*. Molcajetes are volcanic stone gourds where different foods are prepared. One of the most popular is *aguachile*. It consists of lemon, salt and pepper, chile, cucumbers, onion, and raw shrimp, all mixed up in a molcajete. The result is magical. If you ever find yourself in Tijuana, there are a number of infamous local dishes. Sopita de mariscos would be one. Tacos de pescado and marlin would be there. And, of course, ceviche and aguachile. The nice part about it is that they serve you the molcajete along with the food. You can eat the ceviche or aguachile right out of the molcajete.

We walk across the street over to the corner where the restaurant is. Sure enough, Hector is at the bar in "Mariscos El Toreo," but I don't see any seafood in front of him. What I do see is a couple empty bottles of Bohemia in front of him and a tall glass. As soon as I see the Bohemia I want one. I can't sit down fast enough. The bartender serves me one in a glass. The beer is cold, and beads of sweat form on the glass. The Bohemia is smooth, and strong. It always is. I look at the refrigerator behind the bar, and the digital thermostat reads '37' degrees. A good bar always promotes how cold their beer is. A bar that has a thermostat registering the temperature of their beer is a confident establishment. These are the establishments I frequent. There are no debates, arguments, or doubts on how cold the beer is.

"Hector, when did you get here?"

"About two hours ago."

I look at his face.

"Yeah, that looks about right."

With some people it is hard to discern if they are drunk or sober. Other people wear their inebriation on their sleeve. Hector fits the latter description. One look at Hector and you know how much he has had to drink. He is definitely drunk, but I can also tell he hasn't reached for the heavy stuff yet. He's definitely drunk, but in a good way. No tequila or scotch yet. It's a beer buzz, and I can tolerate that. I can catch up.

"Israel, who is this?" Hector asks.

"You're drunk. You know who this is. My girlfriend. Susana."

"Suzie," I chime in.

"You know she doesn't like to be called that, Blake." Israel informs me. I look over at Susana. She stares back. Hector calls her "Suzie-Q."

"Ah, come on. What are you doing?"

"What are you doing? You're drunk."

"*En vino veritas.*"

Susana looks over at me. Israel asks, "What's that?"

"It's Latin. It means 'Truth in Wine'."

Hector is laughing so hard he nearly falls off his chair.

"What's so funny?" Israel asks me.

"I don't know. Ask him," I reply.

"C'mon, let's eat."

I order two tostadas de ceviche. Israel orders a shrimp cocktail. Susana doesn't order anything.

"Aren't you going to eat?"

"I'm not hungry."

Israel leans over.

"She doesn't like seafood."

"Suzie" doesn't like anything. She's the type to sit down in a restaurant and not order anything except water, while everybody else is enjoying their food. Because she can't find one single thing on the menu that she finds edible, she will sit there and not eat anything, making everybody else at the table uncomfortable. I wonder how she goes through life like that.

"Well, I fucking love seafood." I emphasize this, for Susana's sake.

"Who is fighting today?" Israel asks.

"Mauricio, and Amaya. Pablo Hermoso is going to be on the horse."

"What a surprise. Amaya is always in Tijuana."

"He's from Tijuana. Any big fight is going to include him."

"Well, that and his connections. Amaya is familiar with the right people."

I can't keep the pressure off of Susana for too long, so I press.

"Suzie, why don't you like the Bullfights?"

She just shrugs, "Not my scene."

"So, what is your scene?"

Israel gives me a bad look, but I can't help myself. I don't know why he is with her. She drags the whole group down, and that bothers me. I want to harass her; I don't know why. It's perverse, I know it is. But there it is. Poe made a good case for perversity, and I think it applies here. I've got that Imp on my shoulders today.

"We can go somewhere afterwards. Maybe someplace quiet, you know, your scene."

"Blake, back off. She just doesn't enjoy crowds, that's all."

Israel looks visibly annoyed now, so I back off a bit. Susana grates on my nerves, but I respect Israel enough to drop it.

"Alright, alright, it's going to be hard to find a 'quiet' place in Tijuana, that's all."

"Hey, relax."

"Ok, ok, I can relax."

"I can always relax with food like this."

"And on a night like this."

"True, true. When it's hot, in summer, you always need good mariscos and a good corrida de toros."

"And you get it here."

"Learn to enjoy. That's my philosophy on life."

"Well, it's easy to enjoy here, in an environment like this."

"I agree."

"Where's Gaby?" Israel inquires.

"Yeah, where's my cousin?"

I look at them both.

"She's coming. She knows we are here. Don't expect her to be on time, though."

"Yes, I know my cousin. Being on time is not part of her philosophy."

"Really?" Israel asks me, "you came down alone?"

"I wanted to eat here before it starts, and I knew Gaby wasn't going to make it in time. Don't worry; she doesn't mind driving down here."

"When does it start?"

"Normally at four o'clock," I tell him. "However, this is an evening corrida, so it's going to start at six. It's about the only thing that starts on time in Tijuana, or anywhere else in Mexico. A corrida de toros will always start at four o'clock in the afternoon."

"Why does it start on time?"

"I don't know, but it's about the only the thing that does down here. You can count on it."

"Well, we better finish up and grab our seats."

"Yeah, when it gets crowded it's hard to get to your seats. 'El Toreo' always gets that way."

"Why?"

"It's old. All the barreras are wooden," I inform them. "If it's a packed house, you can feel the whole arena sway with the crowd."

"It gets scary. You feel like the whole bullring is about to collapse," Hector adds in.

Susana gets visibly ill at this prospect. I continue for the effect.

"Oh yeah, about two years ago, they sold too many tickets. People were standing everywhere. I could feel the bullring move. It felt like it was going to come down on top of us."

"How old is the bullring?"

"Fifty, sixty years old. Check the wood planks. They looked rotted out."

Suzie shakes her head. "I'm not getting in there if it's sold out. I don't like the looks of it."

"Yeah, I've heard they have been trying to condemn it for years, but they can't. It's considered a cultural landmark of Tijuana."

"Right, until people die in it."

"It won't be a cultural landmark then."

"But supposedly Marilyn Monroe and Eva Gardner have been here to watch a Bullfight. It's historic. That's why they won't get rid of it."

"Why? Israel asks, "they have a better bullring in Playas."

"Yeah, but Playas is a pain in the ass to get to," I inform him. "The traffic is horrendous getting out of there. Plaza El Toreo is extremely convenient. You can catch a cab from anywhere for about five dollars, anywhere in Tijuana."

"True, and you can walk down to the Zona Rio," Hector adds in.

'Who else are we meeting?" Israel asks.

"Adrian and Sonia. They are sitting with us, but you know Adrian."

"Always late."

"I can't figure that one out. He takes longer to get ready than Sonia."

"Yes. If you're waiting on Sonia, it's a half-hour to forty-five minutes. If you're waiting on Adrian it's going to be well over an hour."

"He takes thirty minutes to do his hair."

We are all laughing now.

"Wait, he puts the same stuff in his hair that you do."

Susana actually smiles at this.

"It's true, he uses Murray's."

"No, I thought you used Tiger pomade?"

"Not anymore. Murray's pomade is the best. It certainly lasts the longest."

Hector nods his head, "I don't know how you guys sleep with that stuff in your hair. What happens to your pillow?"

"Yeah, that's definitely a tricky maneuver. But you can do it."

"With a hair net."

"He uses one!" Susana blurts out.

I'm aghast, because Suzie finally made a comment.

"Israel, your girl is outing you."

I get worried that comment went too far, but I observe no reaction from either Israel or Susana. Israel actually plays off it.

"Who cares if I like a good pompadour? Who doesn't now-a-days?"

"My grandpa had one. I should ask my grandma what he used."

"Hank's pomade, the old stuff, probably."

I check my watch. "Let's get going. Adrian and Sonia are going to meet us inside. I don't want to get caught up trying to get to our seats."

"Don't worry, Hector replies, "the Bullfight will start on time, but no Tijuanero will be there on time. It doesn't fill up until half-way through."

"I want to grab some *carne seca* in there. It's the best."

"Alright, let's go."

We walk back across the street to the plaza de toros El Toreo. There are food and drink stands circling the bullring, giving it a festive atmosphere. L.A. Cetto has a tented area, and we make our way there. It should be easy enough to get a table and grab a bottle of wine or two before we head inside. I purchase a bottle, and a wine skin, and pour the wine in the wine skin. It's a tricky maneuver, but I manage to pour my wine in without spilling any. This way, I will be able to enter the bullring with my wine. There are two types of wine skins; there is the one–litre skin, which will hold a bottle of wine, and the five–litre variety. Only a real alcoholic can hold down a five–litre by themselves. I roll with the one–litre, as it whets my appetite. When it's hot, a cold beer is the way to go. When the weather is decent, a bottle of wine can go a long way. There are two bullrings in Tijuana, and I base it off of that. Plaza de Toros El Toreo is located along Boulevard Agua Caliente, in the heart of Tijuana, so it holds to true California weather; always hot in the summer. The plaza de toros in Playas, on the other hand, experiences a different climate. This plaza, one of the finest in Mexico, is right on the beach. It experiences typical 'Playas' weather: perpetual overcast. You can see this as you drive into Playas itself, you will leave sunlight and enter cloudiness as you drive down from La Mesa into the beach area. Playas is notorious for this unique climate. It's always five to ten degrees cooler than the rest of Tijuana. It seems that a marine layer resides over the whole area. A good bottle of wine is always recommended for Playas, a cold bottle of beer is always needed in the sun in plaza El Toreo. However, I switch it up today because I'm in the mood for a little of both.

We walk through the parking lot up to the plaza de toros. We see the advertisements for the Bullfights this weekend, and they are heavily produced. There are three: tonight, Saturday afternoon, and Sunday. Tijuana does this, once a year, to celebrate the anniversary of the city and it is always a big celebration. I personally enjoy it. An entire weekend of bullfights and fun. The Friday night Corrida is unique, they only do it once a year. El Toreo has lights, so they can pull it off. The night Corrida is always the most festive of the lot, because it kicks off the weekend. In July, the days are hot, but the evenings are perfect. We have such a night tonight. There is not a cloud in the sky, and the weather is nice and dry, with a very small breeze coming in from the ocean. We always plan around this, and the social crowd of Tijuana is always out to make a scene. We walk up the staircase to the second level and find our seats. I scan the crowd.

"I don't see her in here. Does Gaby know where we are sitting?"

"Yeah, we always sit in the same place."

"Call her cell phone."

"Ha! She doesn't carry one."

This brings Susana out of her reverie, "What do you mean, she doesn't carry one?"

"That's what I mean. She doesn't carry one. She claims it's a hassle for her. She says if it's really important for you to reach her, you will."

"That's an unusual attitude."

"Well, you can ask her about it when she comes."

"If she comes," Hector adds in.

As soon as he says that I spot Gaby, walking through one of the entranceways to our level. As usual, she is with company. There are two guys and two girls she is with, and she is in the middle of them. All of her guest's attention is focused on her. She is telling some joke, or making some witty remark. They all laugh. She leans over and taps somebody else on the shoulder. It's an older gentleman. He gets up, they embrace, and he introduces them to his group. She introduces her guests. They speak for a few minutes. We are all watching the scene. They embrace again, and she turns back to her group of friends. Finally, she looks up, see us, waves, then goes back to her conversation. They all stop at a cooler to purchase their drinks. They speak for a little bit, then Gaby motions for them to follow her. They do. The two guys bother me. Obviously, only one of them is with the other girls. The other guy, I don't know. That's the way it always is with her. She walks up, all smiles.

"How does the crowd look?" Gaby asks.

"It's going to be packed here tonight," Hector tells her. "I've always wanted to go to an evening bullfight. They have a *Rejoneador* here."

Her friends walk up and she has to introduce them. They sit with us. One of her friends asks me what a *Rejoneador* is. Gaby turns and asks as well. I don't feel like answering, but with everybody looking at me I feel I have to.

"Bullfight on horseback, Portuguese style. If he does it right he can complete the entire *suerte* and kill the bull from the horse. The real scene though is afterwards."

Sonia and Adrian walk up, holding hands. They look like a nice couple. There are a couple of vendors right below our seats, one selling beer out of a larger cooler, one selling food. The carne seca is there, and I order one.

"I always come for the carne seca."

"What's carne seca?" Susana asks.

"Dried strips of meat, with hot sauce. Kind of like beef jerky, but with a Mexican touch. It's much better than beef jerky, though. Want some?"

"No, I'm ok. Give me your wine, I want a taste."

Sonia asks, "Anybody know where Ricardo is?"

"No, he hasn't called Hector or anybody."

"What about you, Evan?"

"What, me? I don't carry a cell phone."

"You're the only guy I know who doesn't."

"I don't like the feeling of being on call twenty-four hours a day."

"He just wants the excuse of avoiding me, that's all."

"Not true, babe, not true. I just don't like them. You can find me if you want to get a hold of me, that's all. And I don't know what the hell you are talking about. You don't own one either."

"I don't believe in them."

"What if it's an emergency?"

"Then deal with the emergency yourself."

"This is what I deal with." I say.

"You guys are two peas in the same pod," Sonia says. "A couple without cell phones. If I didn't know any better I would believe you both were trying to avoid each other." She smiles at me.

"I couldn't stand not having a cell phone, myself," Susana adds in. I ignore her, and focus on Sonia.

"Sonia, I lived most of my life without one. People lived for centuries without one. Believe me; it's not going to kill you not to have a phone on you twenty-four hours a day."

"I don't think I could function without one."

"You could. Believe me, you make do. Why do you think you need one? Who convinced you that you need one?"

"I don't know, nobody I guess. Everybody has one."

"I'm somebody, and I don't have one. Liberate yourself, Sonia. You'll find out how refreshing it is to not carry around a cell phone all day."

"Next time I lose mine, I'll give it a try."

"If somebody really needs to get a hold of you, believe me, they will."

"I can testify to that. And it's a pain in the ass to get a hold of her," Sonia points at Gaby.

"That's the way I like it. That way I know he really cares," Gaby says in my direction.

Everybody laughs at that.

"That's the way Gaby is. Whatever everybody else does, she does the opposite."

"It's my philosophy on life."

Our conversation dies off and our attention focuses back on the bullfight. The Corrida de toros has begun. We watch the first bull enter the ring. The gates wooden gates make a crash against the barrera, and an enormous bull comes storming out. A young Torero by the name of Mauricio comes out to take the bull away. Tijuana is considered a provincial bullring, despite the size of the arena itself. Most bullfighters that perform in Tijuana are young. From time to time, Tijuana will bring in a high profile bullfighter, but not often. The size of the crowd in Tijuana really has nothing to do with the cartel itself. The 'Cartel' is the poster that is plastered all over town, listing the bullfighters that are to be present at the bullfight, along with the name of the ranch where the bulls are coming from. A novice will pay attention only to the names of the bullfighters. An Aficionado will determine a good 'cartel' by the bulls themselves. Different ranches produce different qualities of bulls. It's really the bulls that make the bullfight, not the matadors.

The people of Tijuana come to the bullfights for other reasons; for social reasons. If it's on a holiday weekend, if the weather is good, if the conditions are right, then it will be a big crowd. If unfavorable conditions exist for the bullfight, then the crowd will be small. Most citizens of Tijuana go to a bullfight to be seen, not to watch a spectacle. There are some aficionados, but not many. The scene in Tijuana is too dynamic, fluctuating with the summer. There are very good seasons, and very bad ones. It's a tough business in Tijuana, and it is difficult to make money. I assume most of the money they make is on food and drink sales than it is anything else. The people of Tijuana are too fickle for any concrete fan base to exist. Sonia is an aficionado. So am I. Gaby is not. She's there to run into friends and be seen. Hector goes because everybody else goes. Israel goes because he is invited and he enjoys the spectacle. Adrian goes because Sonia is going and he wants to scope out the scene. Susana is here against her will. Everybody has their reasons, and for the most part it has nothing to do with the bulls or bullfighters. Gaby is in a good mood tonight, which bodes well for me.

"Gaby, what's the plan afterwards?"

"Oh, who knows? You tell me."

'Ok., I can come up with something."

"I'm counting on it."

"I have a room at the Pueblo Amigo. I don't want to be in a position to have to cross the border tonight."

"Yes, and it's going to take us forever to get out of here. We might as well stay the night."

So, it is going to be a good night for me. Gaby told me everything I need to know right there. All of a sudden, I want the corrida to be done and over with. But I have to play along, so I will. Adrian is talking with Israel, and it looks like he is having a good time. Susana brings Israel down a bit, but he insists on dragging her around everywhere. I wonder about this. There is a decent crowd tonight, but it won't reach capacity until about half-way through the corrida. The bullfight is one of the few organized events in Latin America to start on time, but most people of Tijuana don't operate that way. They will pay full price for a ticket and only watch half of the show. Whatever. It's their money. That's the way they operate. It is the *modus operandi* of Tijuana. Wait in line, and be late for everything. There will be a long line to get out of here, but the people accept that here. The good thing about the plaza de toros El Toreo is that is located in the Zona Rio. There are fine restaurants and great bars within walking distance.

"We can walk over to Casa Plasencia, or down to La Cantina de los Remedios."

"Casa Plasencia first. When we get low on money, we can catch a cab someplace else."

Adrian jumps in on our conversation, "Casa Plasencia? Damn, it's expensive in there. Let's go to Ruben Hood."

Gaby is incredulous at this. "Ruben Hood? They shoot people in there. I'm not going in there."

Sonia agrees. "Forget the Ruben Hood. We can go to Cantina."

"Alright, La Cantina it is. Let's enjoy first. We can drink in the tents afterwards."

"Yeah, let's do that. I don't want to go broke too early tonight. But I want to stay for the whole fight. I like that Mauricio guy. He's pretty good," Israel says. Israel is always worried about going broke.

We watch the rest of the corrida in fine spirits. The crowd is decent tonight, and Mauricio cuts a couple of ears. He is very popular in Tijuana, despite his youth. He is a favorite with the women. He is not a bad looking guy. Those tights he wears with his Traje de Luces helps the imagination with the women. Sonia and Gaby want to go down to the exit before the corrida ends, hopefully to score a picture with Mauricio and see if they can chat him up. Most of the young bullfighters are looking to hit the town after a bullfight, and Mauricio is no exception. It takes a special skill to determine where a bullfighter is going to spend his evenings after a corrida de toros, and Gaby and Sonia have that skill. It's almost a sixth sense. Israel originally protests leaving early to go down and catch a glimpse of Mauricio, but when Sonia explains her plans Susana and him are all for it. We walk down from our seats, then walk over to the exit of the bullring, where the Matadors walk out after they finish. The infirmary is right there, ready to provide medical assistance if there are any problems. Nobody receives a horn wound tonight. A few other people, with the same idea are waiting at the exit. I can see the chapel of the bullring over the heads of the crowd. The chapel of the bullring in plaza El Toreo is actually located underneath the stands, nuzzled inside the labyrinth of steel beams that hold the plaza together. It's a bizarre place for a chapel, but it is very old so nobody minds. The Matadors make their way out, along with their retinue, and Gaby and Sonia push their way over to Mauricio. He is very gracious, and takes pictures with anybody that wants one. Hector, Adrian, and myself stand back and watch the proceeding. Israel takes a picture for Sonia and Gaby, then Israel and Susana take a picture with Mauricio. Mauricio is a good looking guy. His hair is slicked back and he is sweaty from the bullfight. Gaby and Sonia have a quick conversation with Mauricio as he is taking other pictures. They seem satisfied, then leave. We walk out to the outside of the bullring to the tents and have a few drinks. Sonia and Adrian seem to be fighting. It might be because of Mauricio. I ask Gaby about it.

"Yeah, they have been fighting lately. Why, I don't know."

"Is it because of that scene with Mauricio just now?"

"Yes, maybe. I don't why he's getting jealous lately. If anybody has reason to be jealous, it's Sonia."

"What? What do you know about it?"

Gaby looks around at our table, but everybody else is engaged in conversation. Israel and Hector are talking to people at the next table. Susana is sitting by herself. Adrian and Sonia are having their own conversation, and they don't seem interested in what everybody else is doing. Gaby leans over to me.

"Some people I know have seen him around Tijuana lately. And he hasn't been with Sonia."

That statement hits a little too close to home. That's the problem with this city. Even though it has big-city dimensions, it has small-town atmosphere. Everybody knows everybody.

"That's the trouble with Tijuana," I say. "You're bound to run into somebody you know down here. It's unavoidable."

"Yes, a few friends have told me. I'm not going to get involved with that. He just doesn't have a right to be jealous, that's all."

"The people that get jealous are always the ones that you need to watch."

"Exactly. A jealous person isn't jealous because of their partner; they're jealous because of themselves. They judge other people by their own actions."

"Don't ever get jealous with me—because I'll know what that means."

"Why do you think I'm here with you? You're never jealous."

"See, I have my advantages."

"Yes, you do."

Gaby has had a few drinks, enough to be frank and honest. I tell Gaby I'm getting tired. It's a lie.

"Yeah, we can leave in a little bit. I don't want to abandon Sonia like this, though."

"Are they crossing back?"

"Yes, I think so."

"Come on, let's get out of here."

"Alright, alright. Hold on."

I walk over to Israel, and Gaby goes with Sonia. We walk in small groups down to La Cantina de los Remedios.

Israel and I have a good conversation about the bullfight. Sonia brags that they found out where Mauricio is going to be afterwards, and they are going to meet him. It bothers me a bit, but I don't let on. It bothers Adrian to no end when he finds out that Mauricio is also going to be in La Cantina.

We walk in and are quickly seated. Many people had the same idea we did, and the restaurant fills up quickly. Hector asks if we want to order food, but I decline. That's too much of a commitment. Instead we order two *cubetas*. There are several groups of musicians circling the tables, looking to play. The table next to us orders a few songs, and we listen in. Then another table orders more songs from another band, and they commence playing. La Cantina can get this way, and it becomes chaotic. There can be three to four different bands playing different music at the same time, and you can hear them all from wherever you sit. I pull a beer out of the bucket and brush off the ice. I grab the bottle opener and open my beer. Gaby leans over to the next table, where her friends from earlier are sitting, and speaks to them. She has to shout to be heard. I drink my beer. Hector is drunk, but holding his own.

"Evan, how about tomorrow?" Hector yells over at me. "Ready for another one?"

"No, I doubt it. Maybe Sunday. The cartel isn't all that impressive tomorrow."

"What? Who cares about the cartel?" he shouts.

"I do," I shout back.

The band playing at the next table start playing louder, and another group a few tables down commences playing.

"Goddammit!" I yell. "I can't hear myself think!"

"What?" Hector asks. "Do you want to go tomorrow or what?"

"I don't think so."

"Whatever. Every fight this weekend is good. They're even bringing in the *Forcados de Mazatlán*."

"Maybe!" I shout. "Let me see what my finances are. We are staying over here tonight."

"See? There you go."

Adrian doesn't say much. Susana has a few things to say, then she's ready to go home. I hope this is my cue to leave. Suzie has her advantages. She's my excuse to cut out early tonight. I tell Suzie I'm getting tired, and she agrees with me. She's tired as well. Israel shoots a dirty look in our direction. I think he was just getting warmed up. Suzie finally gets excited about something. She is anxious to leave. Israel looks away from us. I don't care though, I have other plans that don't involve him. I ask Adrian what they are doing and he shrugs. Israel tries to convince him to go someplace else. Anywhere. He agrees. Adrian and Israel want to continue drinking. I don't. I tell everybody that I am tired. Adrian gets angry at this, but fuck him. Time to take him out of the equation. I have to be pre-emptive. I tell them I have a room at the Pueblo Amigo. Sonia doesn't want us to leave, but Gaby says she is tired as well. That seals it for me. Gaby and I leave arm and arm. I wave good-bye to everybody, and nobody seems happy that we are leaving. I'm not worried. I know they are going for drinks right now. I can miss one night on the town. It won't kill me. I'm happy now. Gaby and I leave for the night.

* * * *

There are a line of taxis waiting in front of Cantina de los Remedios. I hail one and we both climb inside. I inform Gaby that I'm hungry, so we agree to try and find "Mariscos Tony." "Don Tony" opened a small seafood stand on a street-corner in downtown Tijuana. The cart is a typical Tijuana food-cart; it is small and has wheels on the bottom so it remains mobile. It also has a foldable canopy and a battery-run spotlight that serves him in the night. Don Tony's cart is atypical in that Tony serves only sopa de mariscos, or shrimp soup. *Sopa mariscos* is a Tijuana delicacy. The soup is served to you in a cheap styrofoam cup, with corn tortillas on the side. You can drink the soup directly from the cup, eat it out of a spoon, or roll tortillas in your hand and dip the tortillas straight in your soup. The difficulty with "Mariscos Tony" is locating his cart. Although when asked, Tony will insist that he always sets up shop on the same street-corner. I insist that he moves his locations around. His hours are also awkward. During the week he only opens from two in the morning to six in the morning. On the weekends, he extends his operation by opening around midnight.

"Are you sure Don Tony is open right now?" Gaby asks.

"Pretty sure. On Saturdays he opens earlier."

"I hadn't heard that. Normally he doesn't open his cart until two in the morning."

"Well, let's find out. I'll bet you a cup of *sopita* that he's open."

"I'm not buying you soup."

I order the cab to drive down Calle Ocampo, past La Sexta. No sign of the cart.

"Try Calle Madero. One block down. He's usually there, not on this street." Gaby instructs the cab driver.

"I should have called Rafa," I say.

"Who?"

"Nothing, just a cabbie I know."

The driver runs through a stop-sign and turns left on Calle Madero. Gaby points ahead.

"Yeah, a little further down. He's usually behind the Jai Alai. He sets up his cart right on the corner, next to the Cathedral."

A block ahead I see a large church rise up from the ground. There is steam rising from a cart on the side of the street. Gaby was right. Tony looked like he was just setting up shop, which is what I want.

"See, he just opened. The tortillas should be hot."

"I don't care about that." I inform Gaby. "You're not supposed to eat soup with tortillas."

"Evan, that's how I know you're not Mexican. No Mexican would say such a thing. You can eat just about anything with tortillas—including soup."

"I drink my soup. Or eat it out of a spoon."

No, I'm, eating with tortillas. It's the only way to do it."

The cab pulls up right next to the cart, and I ask him if he can wait for us to eat. He replies that he will wait. I give him the fare and a tip and I ask him if he is hungry. He shakes his head no. Don Tony finishes putting on his apron as we walk up. We are his first customers. His cart is small, with a caulderon underneath full of the *sopa*. The tortillas are stacked on the side of the cart. The styrofoam cups are stacked on the other side. Don Tony is ready. I place two orders, and Tony greets me with a smile. He says it's good luck to start the night off so quickly. He serves us our soup and asks us if we desire tortillas. Gaby replies in the affirmative.

"See Evan, this is what you do. You place your tortilla on the palm of your hand—like so." Gaby makes a big exaggeration of placing her tortilla on her hand. "Then, you place your other hand on top, catch the edge with your hand, move your hands across each other, and roll the tortilla. Make sure you roll it nice and tight. That's important. Then you dip in and enjoy."

"Thanks for the class."

"See, now you fit in. Tony will respect you more if you roll your tortillas. It's the only way to do it down here."

At hearing his name, Don Tony points at Gaby's tortilla and looks at me, giving his approval. My way of eating sopita de camaron is acceptable, but not approved. I tell Gaby that I'm a paying customer and that I can eat it any way I see fit. Don Tony agrees, but informs me that there are always different ways to do certain things, and some ways are better than others.

"If this guy keeps giving me attitude I'm not coming here again."

"Whatever," Gaby laughs. "You'll be back here no later than next week, and you know it."

I take a spoonful of my soup and agree with her. Gaby quickly tells something in Spanish to Tony and they both chuckle. I take a drink of my soup and swallow a piece of shrimp. The soup is spicy, but not too hot. The soup has spices, but is not over-spiced. The soup has the smell of seafood, but is not too heavy. The *sopita de camaron* is well balanced. Don Tony has mastered his ingredients, and for forty pesos you can sample his mastery. In my mind, it is a bargain.

"Gaby, ask him why he keeps such odd hours. Why doesn't he open during the day?"

"Who cares? He's smart, that's all. He caters to the drunk crowd and the working stiffs at the same time. Mariscos is always good to prevent a hang-over, and the sopita is a decent breakfast as well."

"True."

"Tony, when do you start getting busy?" I ask.

"A las tres, cuatro en la mañana," he replies.

"Dandy's del Sur hours."

Gaby looks at me after the last comment.

"What do you mean by that?"

"That's when Dandy's gets busy as well."

"Oh, your special dive-bar."

"That's right."

We finish our soup, Gaby walks around the cart to give Tony a hug, and I pay the bill with a tip. I make sure to tip Tony well, because I will be back. As we walk back to the cab, another couple and a group of noisy girls are making their way to Tony's cart. I get that drowsiness after eating greasy food, and Gaby gives me that look. I open the door for her and we both climb in the back seat.

"A dónde?" our driver asks us.

I look over at Gaby.

"Wherever," she tells me.

"Pueblo Amigo," I inform the driver.

We make our way to Paseo de los Heroes and over the bridge to the Palacio Municipal. From the Palacio it's just down the street to the Pueblo Amigo. We stop at a bar across the street from the hotel and have one last drink. The night is over before it really began.

X

The summer turned hot, and humid, which was unexpected in Southern California. It can be hot, but normally the heat is a dry heat from the desert. Dry heat is bearable, humidity is not. Being a native of Southern California, I don't know how people of other parts of the country deal with humidity. I can be comfortable in ninety–degree weather if it is dry enough. I cannot deal with humidity at any level. I sweat at night. I sweat during the day. I shower two, three times a day, just to get comfortable. The problem was a storm was blowing in from the south, over the Sea of Cortez. The California coast has a cold current running down from Alaska all the way down the Baja Peninsula, so any wind or weather from the Northern Pacific is cool and dry. This current moderates California weather. However, when the weather turns and we get winds from the south, it is full of humidity and thunder-showers. Weather from the Sea of Cortez has a tropical quality to it. I had been a week in San Diego spending time with family, eating with Gaby, visiting Tijuana occasionally, when Israel called and said he wanted to get out of town for a day or two. I was agreeable. If nothing else, maybe I could beat the weather by getting out of town for a stretch. I worked through the week, put in as much overtime as they would give me, had lunch with my co-worker Rick, and prepared for a weekend off. Rick asked where I was going, and I replied, "Baja." He told me he wanted to come, but his family obligations did not permit it. I told him I understood. I asked him to put in a word for me about an extra shift or two during the week. He replied that he would make it happen. I put in as much overtime as I could for a few extra dollars in my pocket. I enjoy putting my head down and working hard for a week or two straight. The pay-off is when you get that payroll check. Then it's time to enjoy. It's a simple relationship: hard work followed by enjoyment. I've put it my time for two weeks, now it's time to enjoy.

The plan was settled: Ensenada. It was Israel Duarte, Ricardo and Eddie Tellez, and myself. Hector Tellez agreed to meet us down there if he can get off of work. The best of company, by my standards, and without any entanglements. The question was what to do once we arrived, but there are only a few options down there. The drive down to Ensenada is nice; it always is. The road is a toll road, but I don't mind paying the fare down. It's not that expensive, and the trade off is a nice, two lane highway. The drive is always smooth, once you get out of Playas. The toll road begins in Playas, then it is a straight shot down to Ensenada. A car full of friends makes the ride go by quickly. We stop at an Oxxo, pick up some beer, and enjoy the ride down with a beer in our hands. It feels nice to drive while drinking a beer, with the window pulled down and a nice ocean breeze coming in through the window. I don't mind driving; I never do. I could have been a truck driver, no problem. I can almost meditate while I'm driving. I get in a lot of good daydreaming while I drive. Hours on the road don't faze me a bit. A convertible would have been perfect here, but I don't have one. I want one, however.

Drinking while driving is perfectly acceptable on this road, with minimal consequences. If you can avoid it, don't get pulled over. If you do, nothing to panic over. There will be no jail time involved, but a payoff will be in order. Police-work south of the border has an entrepreneurial spirit about it. Frankly, the beat cops don't make enough money to survive down here, so they have to find other sources of revenue. Corruption has a different connotation here. A police officer that pulls somebody over for speeding and takes a twenty dollar bill for his troubles is not considered corrupt. You should not view it as so. To him or her, that's breakfast money for doing his or her job. The police officer that takes money from drug cartels to ignore certain things could be considered corrupt. Ignoring drug trafficking is not part of the job description. Pulling over speeders is. Taking money for doing his job is not in itself corrupt. This understanding will take you a long way in any dealings with the authorities down here. It's just a different set of circumstances and situations, that's all. My finances are limited. I have enough to do what I want to do, but not much more. I don't want to be set back when I'm just beginning the weekend, so I instruct my fellows to keep the beer out of sight. I don't mind them drinking, however. It's easy to spot police officers coming up behind you, so I don't worry so much. I just keep an eye on my mirrors so our trip isn't hampered prematurely. Ricardo asks us what the plan is, and we all respond. There are only so many things to do in Ensenada.

"Hussong's, and the *Mercado Negro.*"

"What the hell is 'Hussongs'?" Eddie asks.

"It's a bar; the oldest bar in Baja. It was opened by some German immigrants. Good bar. If you need a good beer in Ensenada, Hussong's is the place to go. It's an old fashioned cantina."

"What about the *Mercado Negro?*"

"That's Spanish for 'Black Market.' "

"What's on the Black Market?"

"Eddie, relax!" Ricardo exclaims. "My brother asks too many questions. It's due to his youth and inexperience," he tells me.

"Don't worry Eddie," I tell him. "It's not really a black market, just a large area full of seafood restaurants and stands, right off the wharf in Ensenada."

As always, it's not the locations *per se*, but the company that determines success or failure in any outing. I am with good company today. I can already spot a recipe for success. Eduardo is an unusual case. He practically grew up around adults. No friends his age at all. You will find Eddie much to mature for his age, able to opine on a number of subjects. Eddie can hold a conversation with the best of them. Eduardo Tellez is more comfortable around older adults than people his own age. Other than that, he's the most down–to–earth guy I know.

"What happened to Gaby?"

"Couldn't make it. And to tell you the truth, I'm glad that she couldn't. I've had enough of that for awhile."

"What's awhile?" Eddie asks, laughing.

"Probably as soon as I get back."

"That sounds about right."

"But to hell with that, for now. I'm down here this weekend, so let's enjoy."

"Here, here." Ricardo slams his beer mug with each 'here' for emphasis.

"Ok, so where to?"

Ricardo blurts, "Well, there's this first-rate strip club just down Avenida Macheros. I like the place because they have this glass wall looking into the stripper's dressing room. You can see them change and everything."

"I've never heard of that before," Israel states.

"Me neither," Ricardo answers. "That's why I like it. But I'm hungry. Let's eat first."

"Mercado Negro, then. Shoot, that's why I came down here."

"Tijuana stole it's style from the Mercado Negro. They perfected the fish taco and the marlin taco and the tostada de ceviche long before Tijuana did."

"Whoever came up with cooking fish in lime juice was a fucking genius."

"Yeah, it's a Baja specialty."

"What do you mean, 'cooked in lime juice'?"

"Ceviche is raw fish and shrimp. They just let it sit in lime juice, along with a few other ingredients."

"I had no clue I was eating sushi."

"No, it's not exactly sushi. It's just prepared different-ly. The lime takes away from the fishiness. The acidity 'cooks' it. Then mix in diced tomatoes, onions, cilantro, a few spices, and there you go."

"Cold ceviche is best on a hot day."

"You can't eat it when it's cold out. It doesn't work that way."

"I agree. It tastes different."

On a hot summer day, a table in the Mercado Negro can be hard to come by. As soon as you drive into Ensenada, the Mercado Negro is right off the highway. We drive in, park, and make our way into the market. We wind our way through the crowd to find some empty seats. Down one lane we stumble upon a small bar where the previous group just vacated. The bar is inside and they have a ceiling-fan running. I sit down and wave to the waiter. He walks around to the bar to take my order.

"Dos tacos de marlin, y tres cheves."

"¿Que tipo?"

"Pacifico," I reply.

"¿Y tres vasos?" the bartender asks.

"No, un vaso."

Ricardo turns and laughs, and makes his own order, "Dos tostadas de ceviche."

"¿Pescado, camarón, o mixto?"

"Pescado, y tres cheves también."

The bartender looks at him. "¿Y un vaso?"

"Claro que sí."

The bartender holds his stare at us for a second or two before he turns around to grab our bottles. Israel and Eduardo make their own orders, and we sit down to eat. The Mercado Negro has a good mixture today; families out for the day with their kids, young people out for a tostada and a few beers, vendors all around selling anything they can. The breeze is coming off the ocean, so it keeps the market nice and cool even on the warmest of days. I can smell the brine off the salt water, and the fishy smell of a wharf. It adds to the flavor of the place. The market is packed in today, and it adds to the ambiance. When you go someplace to eat, you want it to be crowded. It gives the food you are eating a validation of sorts. Try eating at a place that's empty one time, and see how you feel about the food. It's never the same. The Mercado Negro has energy today, so I know our food will be good, and the beer cold. The bartender returns with our food, and Israel is the first one to observe and ask, "Why are we ordering three beers with one glass?"

Ricardo countered, "What, you can't handle three beers quickly?"

The man serving us looks visibly nervous, which was strange, because we haven't gotten seriously into our drink yet. Maybe they're not used to bizarre behavior at three in the afternoon.

The waiter brings Ricardo his ceviche on tostadas. He immediately throws hot-sauce all over them. My tacos also arrive. I avoid the hot-sauce. I can smell the cooked marlin. The others order ceviche de camarón.

"I'm surprised they didn't offer us a bucket of beers."

"No, it's just we were too stupid to ask."

"Evan here has to order three beers and one glass, and Ricardo has to match it. That's what led to this."

"Eduardo, you have a point. Next round, lets order a *cubeta*."

We start to dig in our food, but Eduardo has something on his mind, and it's obvious.

"Evan, what about this Gaby business? What's up with you and my cousin?"

"I don't know. The truth is I can't figure her out. The longer I'm with her, the worse it gets."

"We could have told you that, years ago."

"Any woman is like that."

"No, not every woman. Sonia doesn't give any trouble."

"Yeah, but she's our sister, so you better say that."

"With Gaby, I don't know," I tell them. "Whenever it feels right, things go bad. When it goes bad, things get right again."

"She has a hard time committing."

"Why?"

"She's always been like that," Eddie says. "She's my cousin and I love her, but she's flakey. She's also headstrong. She doesn't know what she wants."

"If somebody doesn't know what they want, it's useless."

"If I'm ready to break it off, she'll be ready to move forward."

"Yeah, don't push it. When you want something, you never get it. When you quit worrying about it, it will happen."

"Why not just move on?"

"Don't think I haven't considered it."

And I have thought about it. It's an easy decision for me when I'm separated from her. Sure, make a clean break, and get on with my life. As soon as I see her though, it's a different story. I can't pull the trigger. It's easy enough advice to take. The follow through is the difficult part. Everybody always has good advice. Taking advice is a different skill; one I haven't mastered yet.

"What, you think she'll take it too bad?" Ricardo asks.

"No, the opposite. I don't think she will mind at all. And that's what bothers me."

"Alright, fuck it," Eddie says. "Forget I asked. Let's knock down some brews and forget about it."

"Eddie, you've got wisdom for a swabbie."

We call Eduardo, or Eddie, "swabbie," because of his age. He is the lowest man on the totem pole, but still part of the team. If we were on a ship, he would be swabbing decks.

"So, what's the plan?" Ricardo asks.

"I say we finish here, hit up Hussong's, then hit up that strip club you've been talking about."

"Let's get to it."

※ ※ ※ ※

Ensenada is a beautiful pedestrian city. We walk along Avenida López-Mateos, stopping at a few shops along the way. These stores sell the typical tourist gim-cracks. Israel purchases a Lucha Libre mask. It is red, with a gold outline and a heart on the side. He explains to me that the luchador that wears the mask is named "Mil Mascaras." The trend catches on, and Eddie buys himself a "Blue Demon" mask. They inform me that only the classic luchador masks will do. I reply that I'm fine with that, and give the lady ten dollars for a "Santo" mask. Ricardo refuses to follow along, and informs us that we are wasting our money. I tell him that he is just waiting for later tonight to waste his money on a few strippers. He replies that he will get better value out of his money than I will with mine. I don't argue with him. On the corner of the street a vendor is selling *tejuino* out of a cart. I give the vendor thirty pesos and he hands me a large cup of *tejuino*. I grab a spoon from the cart to mix in the ice-cream with the tejuino. Israel asks me for some, and it gets passed around. The *tejuino* is ice-cold. It is refreshing on a day like this. We take a seat on a bench pushed up against the wall of a small restaurant. We pass the tejuino back and forth as the pedestrian traffic flows in front of us. Some people appear busier than others, but the pace is much more relaxed here. I lean my head against the wall and enjoy the view. The air is fresh and clean down here. People walk by and take no notice of us. Nobody appears to be in a rush. Ensenada has a tranquility that I respect.

"You know, Ensenada is not a bad place. A person could make a good life for himself down here."

"I agree. It's very self-contained. Not too busy, you don't feel rushed like you do in Tijuana."

"Is there work down here?" Israel asks.

"Some. Also, the commute isn't bad. Shoot, some people commute to San Diego from here."

"Yeah, if the border wasn't always a fucking nightmare it wouldn't be a bad drive." Ricardo quips.

Ensenada has a nice downtown area; a good tourist district as well. The Mercado Negro is part of that. There are beautiful houses as you pull in from the coast. You can see them up on the hill, overlooking Ensenada. Also, the weather is Southern California weather. Ensenada isn't far enough down the Baja peninsula to hit that desert weather. Further south, in Mulegé or Loreto, it is downright unpleasant most of the year. Ensenada is far enough north on the Pacific side to avoid that.

"I wonder how much a house costs up there."

"Plenty, I'm sure. There's some money here. Up the corridor as well."

Ricardo makes his way up the street and walks into a small, cramped little bar. It is Hussong's Cantina. It's cramped because it is an old establishment. For some reason, they didn't account for space back in the day. We catch up to him and take a seat at the bar.

"What are you drinking?" I ask Ricardo.

"A beer called 'Indio'. It's a dark beer, with some kick."

Ricardo always goes for the dark beer, wherever he can find it. In San Diego, we refer to those people as 'hopheads.' However, I am not in the mood for a dark beer. I need something lighter today.

"Modelo Especial, por favor."

The bartender serves me my beer in the bottle.

"I wonder when Ensenada is going to get its own micro-brew?" Israel asks.

"They don't need it. The wine scene is blowing up around here. Valle de Guadalupe is going to be huge," I reply.

"L.A. Cetto isn't bad. They produce a good bottle of wine."

"You want one?"

"What, here? You can't order wine in Hussong's. They'll kick your ass all the way out of town."

"True. I'm not in the mood, anyway," I say. "Wine slows you down. I need a pick–me–up."

"Alcohol is all the same, Blake; it's a depressant," Israel says. "Any alcohol will slow you down."

"Beer doesn't slow me down. A good Pale Ale doesn't slow me down."

"Yeah, I'd go for a Sculpin right now!"

We all laugh at Eddie. He has perfect timing.

"I feel like I've been drinking with you forever," Israel tells Eduardo. "How old are you again?"

"Twenty-two."

"Damn, you must have started at about sixteen then."

"With brothers like mine, it was unavoidable."

"That sounds right."

I ask the bartender if he has any Pale Ale from San Diego. He replies that he does.

"Stone?"

"Yes."

"Stone IPA please."

Eddie shakes his head, "Any IPA that is exported from San Diego is automatically Stone. What the hell?"

"I know," Israel says. "They're the oldest; they have the most resources."

"Stone's not bad, but Green Flash is better."

"Green Flash is not better. I'd take Stone over Green Flash any day."

"You're crazy. I would drink Ale-Smith over both of those."

Ok. That's not so crazy. Ale-Smith is not bad."

"Yes, but they're not exporting yet. You can only get a Green Flash or Ale-Smith in San Diego. Stone's the only micro-brew from San Diego you are going to get anywhere else."

"Well, I guess I can go with a Stone. Do they have any Arrogant Bastard?"

"Maybe, but they have the Pale Ale. It's manageable."

"It is."

Hussong's is a must for anybody visiting Ensenada. It has Old World charm. I look around for a jukebox, but decide against it. Usually in a bar such as this, you won't hear the music you selected for a few hours. Too many people piling up.

"Eddie, what the hell are you going to do with yourself?" Ricardo asks.

"Once I finish school, I don't know. We'll see. I need a job."

"You're not going to go on to grad school?"

"Probably not, unless it benefits me. However, a Bachelor's is nothing now. Not the way it used to be. Everybody has a Bachelor's now."

"That's bull," I tell him. "It's always something else. They tell you that you need to go to College. Then they tell you that a Bachelor's degree is a dime a dozen. Go get your Master's. But spend fifty grand in the process."

"Oh, it's a business like everything else. It also feels like a scam. You have to spend all this money just to get your degrees, but nothing is guaranteed."

"Yep, amass a debt just to get a decent job, then spend the next decade working it off. I guess it pays off in the long run."

"That's what they tell you. I get some grants, but it's mostly loans. Loans you have to pay off."

"I never bought into that. It's always something else you have to get, before you can make any money. Believe me, somebody is making money."

"The argument is that it's an investment," Eddie says, "an investment in your future. Whatever. You won't be financially solvent until you turn forty."

"Yeah, and who knows what the market is going to be like when you get there. When we turn forty, they're going to tell us that the only ticket is to get your Ph.D. I don't know what they can tell you after that."

"We're becoming a generation of professional students. Not that it's a bad thing, but can you survive like that?" Eddie asks.

"Why not?" I tell him. "You know most kids now take six to eight years to graduate."

"So? Why not? It's a good life being a student, living off of financial aid," Eddie informs us. "Nobody in college wants to get out into to the real world."

Eddie continues, "Professional student, who doesn't want to get a real job. And why would they? I love what I'm doing right now. I don't want to graduate. Then what? Get a forty–hour, Monday to Friday job? Nothing beats this. Holiday breaks, summers off, and it all gets paid for, one way or another."

"Eddie, you have the life. String it out as long as possible," Ricardo tells him.

"I intend to. I just worry how much I'm racking up in loans, that's all. But that's all down the road. It's all good for me right now. And I have brothers right here buying beer for me, because I'm a poor struggling student."

Ricardo takes offense to this.

"You should be buying me beer, not the other way around."

"You should have went to college. Not my fault."

"Next round is on you."

"Eduardo, you don't know how good you have it. That's the beauty of American culture. They are paying you to go to school. No other country would do that." Israel informs him. "However, if you want to know how it feels to be a real man, let me know. I'll set up a job in construction for you. I'll put your ass right to work."

"No thanks," Eddie replies. We all laugh at that.

'Don't leave school," I tell him.

"I know. It is a good gig."

There is the American Dream in action. Go to school, and get paid to do it. You might amass an enormous debt doing it, but that's part of the American Dream as well. The Dream and debt go hand–in–hand. You want a beautiful house with a picket fence? You can have one, but you also have to take out a loan and pay a mortgage for the next thirty years. In the equation of life in the United States, it's take what you want, but spend your life paying it back. Debt is part of the equation. And it's a conscious choice to play the game. The system is designed that way. Once you're in, once you accrue that debt for a piece of the American Dream, you're all-in. All of your chips are on the table. And the house is going to take its cut, one way or another.

For most people, it's the only way to play. I've never been interested in a game where the stakes are set against me.

The only way to do it is go to a University where the reputation sells. You need an Ivy League education, or something right up there. Hector has a well paying job, but then again he graduated from Berkeley. Gaby and Eduardo are University of California students, so they have a shot at something decent. The rest of us need to learn a trade or else. Ricardo threw his hat in years ago, trying to make it as a musician. His band had some success, then broke up. Israel was a bit smarter, he never bothered with college, other than a few trade classes. Straight to construction; and now he works with cement. Tough job, but once you learn the trade they start paying you well. Israel always works hard, and he's tight with his money, which means he has money. Cheap people aren't cheap because they are broke, they're cheap because they manage their money. Israel is about as stingiest a guy as I have met, but he never runs dry. Israel is slick about it though—it's hard to catch him in the act. If people are buying rounds, he will always buy last, and his turn never comes up twice. If we all chip in for the bill, if Israel is involved the bill will always come up short. He never carries cash; he is always paying with his card. It's good excuse when you don't carry cash. I've seen him in action over the years, and he squirrels away his money with the best of them. He can spend twenty to forty dollars less than everybody else on a given night, and nobody will be the wiser. I keep tabs on him though, and I know his game.

The poorer a person is, the more liberal they are with their spending habits. I've seen this in action in bars all over San Diego. The flashy big tippers will always be tapped out by the end of the night. The real high-rollers are always low-key. They leave a decent tip, and not more. No need to show off; they know they have money. The broke guy needs to show everybody he has money, even when he doesn't. Especially when he doesn't. Rick pointed this out to me one time, and it as close to a universal truth as I have uncovered. The poor guy will tip big early, then shut off at the end of the night. The customer that is flush will tip slow and steady throughout the night, and if you have played your cards right he will tip big in the end. I always listen to Rick. That guy knows what the hell he is talking about.

* * * *

Ensenada is a sanctuary against Tijuana. Just come on down if you ever need a break, and the drive isn't bad. The cruise ships make port here, but the tourists can only spend an hour or two here. That's ridiculous. I've never taken a cruise. If I go somewhere, I want to feel as if I've been there. You can't get a feel for a place in an hour or two. A friend once told me a cruise is all about what happens on the ship, not off of it. Making port is a formality, a requirement. Which is too bad. They could have just as good a time off the ship as on it. I ask the bartender when the next cruise ship is coming in. He replies tomorrow.

"We don't want to be around the tourist zones tomorrow. Cruise ship is coming in."

"Drunk Americans and Canadians."

"Let's go down to La Bufadora tomorrow."

"If we wake up in time."

"Yeah, that's a big 'if.' "

"If we get up too late, we can stop at 'La Fonda' instead."

"Evan, you always want to go to the 'La Fonda,' " Israel chides me.

"I like that hotel," I tell him. "It's a nice spot, and far enough away from the cruise terminal to avoid the tourists."

A lot of people take cruises and then claim they have been somewhere. Two hours isn't enough to brag about. I know plenty of people that claim to have been to Mexico, or the Caribbean. When I find out that it was on a cruise ship, it changes my opinion of them. Taking a cruise doesn't count. You took a cruise—just say that. Two hours making port in some Mexican village doesn't justify as having 'been there.' I don't buy that.

"Ricardo, any gigs lately?"

"No, my scene is gone in Tijuana. When Güereña died, that was it. People don't realize, but he was the driving force. He made everything happen."

"What happened to him?" I ask.

"He died," Ricardo says. "Probably drugs, but who knows. They found him dead in his own house. It was a heart-attack. At the end, he was short on funds."

"That hurt—when he disappeared," Eddie says.

"Yeah, but the punk scene was disappearing in Tijuana anyway. Tijuana No broke up; we broke up. Then Tijuana got crazy, even by Tijuana standards. Bands stop playing in there. They boycotted the city because of the crowds. The people got too wild. They started tearing up venues."

"Oh, like Manu's show in the Auditorio?"

"Yeah, that was definitely one of them. They tore the floor-boards out, then started crowd surfing with them. Thousands of dollars in damage."

"I remember that one. That was the first concert I ever went to. I got punched in the face," said Eddie.

"So what happened?"

"Venues stopped holding shows, and bands didn't want to play anyway. People started getting hurt, so they stopped. Some bands actually boycotted Tijuana for awhile. They refused to play there. There was a lot going on at that time. Güereña wanted to keep going, though."

"But he was bringing in some good acts to Tijuana," I tell him.

"Oh, yeah. He brought in Mudhoney. He brought in The Dead Kennedys. What he would do was pick these guys up after their gig in San Diego, then the next day they would play in Iguanas. That was his deal. He would bring in the best punk bands playing in San Diego and get them a show in Tijuana. Iguanas was the only game in town."

"Didn't he bring in Nirvana?" Israel asks.

"Yeah, but nobody knew who they were back then," Ricardo informs us. "Don't believe anybody who says they saw Nirvana in Tijuana. Güereña said that only about fifty people showed up to that show."

"Shoot, I know two hundred people that claim to have been at that show."

"Yeah, don't believe them. Fifty people—max," Ricardo says. "People give me grief for not being there, but I always say the same thing: Nobody knew who they were."

"Iguana's was a good place."

"Yeah, excellent venue."

"Too bad, because it's a discoteque now."

"Another bawdy Tijuana dance club."

"What's it called now?"

"Who the hell knows. They change the name once a year."

"I think it's called 'Balak—"

"—No, it's called 'Zool.' "

"No, 'Balak.' "

"Who the hell cares. They should just name it 'Another Lame-ass Club for Stupid Drunk Teenagers' and leave it at that."

"Yeah, like Tijuana needs more of those."

"Bring back Iguana's."

Iguana's holds a legendary status in Tijuana. They held some great shows in their day, including Nirvana, Rage Against the Machine, Dead Kennedys, Mudhoney, etc. It doesn't exist now, closed down to make room for another raunchy Tijuana discothèque, full of drunk teenagers. Iguanas in its prime was a real venue. Nothing like it exists now. It was originally designed solely as a music venue, and it was one of the Tijuana greats. It had three different levels, all with a view of the main stage. It had a bar on each level, depending on what ticket you purchased. Iguana's was one of a kind when it opened up, and the music scene opened up with it. Tijuana had a very brief musical revolution, and that movement died with it. I've never seen a movement tied into a venue, but that's exactly what happened. It only stayed open a few years, but those were the golden years. It was the place to be, and the best of the best on either side of the border played there. Iguana's was the center of the universe for a time, but like all good things it came to an end. Nothing in Tijuana lasts.

"Ricardo, did you ever play at Iguanas?" Israel asks.

"Of course. Everybody did. Güereña was a big fan of ours. We met at Iguana's."

"He was a good guy," Eddie quipped.

"No, not all of the time," Ricardo informs us, "sometimes he could be a pain in the ass. He was always working some angle. He was good at getting what he wanted. When he formed Tijuana No, he could barely play an instrument. He just wanted a band. So he collected some local musicians and got it together."

"He couldn't play?"

"He played a little. I mean, he played some keyboard, some percussions, and of course he sang. He wrote some songs. He just wanted to be involved, that's all."

"He got Julieta Venegas?"

"Yeah, but they didn't get along. That's why she left. She was an original band member. She wrote their biggest hit. Güereña didn't get along with her, though. He was a hard guy to get along with, period."

"Yeah, he was a complicated guy."

"Dedicated to the music scene, though. And his house—"

"—Evan, didn't you go there once?" Israel asked me.

"Yeah, once with Ricardo and Hector. He lived right in Zona Norte. You crossed the street and you were in Coahuila."

"Dude, what a house. I can't believe he lived in La Coahuila."

"I can't believe anybody would live there."

"Yeah, any house under a parking lot is unique."

"What?"

"His house was partly under a parking lot."

Ricardo chimed in, "Yeah, and right next to an electricity plant. He never paid for electricity in Tijuana. He had his house illegally wired."

"Only in Tijuana."

"Yeah, it was also a drug den."

"That's where they found him. Dead, in his own house."

'Where did he live?"

"Across the street from La Coahuila. The house was crazy. Houses in Tijuana can be built any which way. You only see houses like that down there."

"And he never paid for electricity?"

"Nope. He wired it. And he lived in Zona Norte."

"He was a Tijuana original, that's for sure."

"He *lived* in Zona Norte."

"Yeah, the most fucked-up *Colonia* in Tijuana, and that's saying something."

"Hey, Zona Norte has its fine points."

"Like what?"

"That baseball field."

"What baseball field?"

"The one right next to the *Internacional*."

"Ok. Other than that?"
"Alright, that may be it."

XI

Our hotel is located right in downtown Ensenada, so it is easy walking distance almost everywhere that is of concern to us. Walking distance is important when you are drunk. There are cabs in Ensenada, which also helps. That's one of the advantages of Mexico; the cabs are a good bargain. They help the drunks. They get you around, and keep you out of trouble. A cab is damned expensive in California. There is no value in them. In Mexico, there is value in taking a cab.

Ensenada doesn't have much of a red light district, but I like that. Ensenada is a place you would want to live. There's not a lot of trouble to go around in this town. They also have decent wines coming out of Valle de Guadalupe, which adds to the flavor of Ensenada. The vibe is different here than the vibe in Tijuana, and I appreciate it. The fishing also isn't bad. It's better further south, but the fishing is acceptable up here as well. As you travel further south, the fishing improves. It's not bad in Ensenada, though. Plenty of boats will take you out. It's hard to pull in a Marlin, even in season, but you can catch plenty of everything else. The Marlin is hard to come by. If you head south, all the way down to Cabo San Lucas, you can catch a Marlin almost anytime, in-season, of course. Ricardo asks if we can go fishing, but I tell him that it is still too early in the summer for good fishing. Later, in the fall, it will get better. Not now. I don't want to rent a boat now. It is not worth it. We will pay a couple hundred dollars, and we might not catch much. The value of things is the key. You must know the values. There is no value right now in deep sea fishing. It is the wrong time of year. But I enjoy coming to Ensenada. Hussong's is the place to go. But any restaurant will do. We are in one now, called 'La Corriente Cevicheria," and they have a good happy-hour. That's why we are here. They have a happy-hour until closing.

"Maybe next time we should give Valle de Guadalupe a shot. I wouldn't mind wine tasting."

"Yeah, I wouldn't either. And they're building a new highway out there. It's supposed to be beautiful."

"You haven't been out there, Evan?"

"No, but Gaby has. I think Sonia has. I'm sure Hector has been there."

"I have," Israel claims.

"Well?"

"Definitely worth it. It's certainly much cheaper than wine tasting in Napa. There are a few decent vineyards out there. We should give it a shot."

"Too late this weekend."

"Actually, they hold a 'Vendimia' in September, to celebrate the end of the grape harvest. It's always a big event."

"Ok., Vendimia sounds interesting."

"Yes, plenty of food, plenty of wine."

"That's the place for me."

Valle de Guadalupe started off small, with only one or two vineyards—L.A. Cetto being one of them. It has grown over the years, partially due to its proximity to the border. There is a small road that leads from Tecate to Ensenada, and that is where the Valle is located. Going in from Tecate is actually a good idea if you are looking to avoid traffic. Most people take the Ensenada route. The Valle is nestled in among some large hills, so it's an oasis of sorts up against the Baja desert. If you want to know how Napa Valley was before it got big and expensive, Valle de Guadalupe is probably as close as you can get. It's a great option if you are a serious wine connoisseur, and it's not overrun by tourists…yet.

We continue our conversation, then move on to other things. The rest of the night goes by quickly. It always does when the conversation is pleasant and there is plenty to drink. We end up closing the bar.

* * * *

We wake up early in the morning and check out of our motel. There is no rush to get the border. Sunday is always the worst day to cross, and we know it. So we don't worry about it. It's going to be about four hours to cross no matter what. We can take our time, eat a good breakfast, have a morning beer or two, and make our way up in the afternoon. We check out around noon, and find a good restaurant to eat breakfast. "Las Tres Pasitas" is our choice, and I eat a plate of huevos rancheros. Our conversation is good, as it has to be. Eduardo is in excellent form. I knew it was the right idea to bring him along. Ricardo, my oldest friend of the bunch, is also doing well. He has had drinks, but not gotten drunk. He has a problem with alcohol, like we all do, and like any good alcoholic he takes it a step too far sometimes. He didn't this weekend, and I appreciate him for it. He recognized the opportunity for a good weekend, and he took advantage. Our breakfast was good; one of the best ones I have had in a long time. I have a michelada with my eggs. It is a good drink with breakfast. The weekend was good, and it was time for us to leave. As we drive up, we make a pit stop at the Hotel La Fonda. It is a mandatory pit stop for us, because it has one of the greatest bars I know. I love this bar. I insist that we stop, and everybody agrees. We've been driving for twenty minutes now, and it is time for a drink. La Fonda is right off the highway on the Pacific Coast side, so I pull off and drive into the parking lot in front. The lot is crowded, which must mean that the hotel is having a good weekend. We all walk inside and grab seats at the bar. It is early enough that there are still plenty of empty bar-stools.

"What is it about this hotel?"

"The bar," I say. "And the view."

The bar has chili-pepper Christmas lights decorating it, and it adds to the flavor. The ceiling is low, and the lighting adds to the ambiance. The hotel sits on a cliff, so every window faces the Pacific. The light from the ocean in the back gives it atmosphere. It's a great place to spend some time. Gaby and I spent a weekend here, when I first met her. It was just the two of us, and it felt like a honeymoon. We spent time on the beach, at the restaurant, and at the bar. That was it. That weekend happened a few years ago, but it feels like a lifetime has passed by. Whenever I walk in here, I always have positive vibrations. That's why I insist on coming back, always.

"I don't know, but it's something about this bar."

"It's long, and wide. You need your space when you sit at a bar. This bar has it."

"Yes, and I like it."

We drink our beers in silence. But the silence is not a problem. Sometimes, silence between friends can be damaging. With us, it is refreshing. Nobody has to say anything. Finally, Ricardo breaks it.

"So, what's happening when we get back?"

"I have to go back up to Santa Barbara," Eddie informs us.

"Back to the mad-house?" I ask.

"Yeah, back to Isla Vista."

Ricardo turns to me, "Evan, what's up with you?"

"I don't know. Keep working. I haven't decided what I'm going to do yet. I don't really want to go back."

"Yeah, but we all have to."

"But nobody wants to."

"That's the ironic part."

"I know."

"We all have to go back to something."

"But you don't have to like it."

"It's better like this."

"It is."

Israel leans back and signals the bartender for another beer. We all follow suit. We have time for one more. I lean over to Eddie.

"Hey, if you can make it down in a few weeks we're all going to the Palenque. You would enjoy it."

Ricardo hears me. "Palenque? I'm down for that."

"Everybody is invited." I say.

"Ok. I'll try. Summer-school is almost over. Maybe I can leave early."

"It's worth it."

We drink our beers slowly this time. Then we order two rounds to go. We ask the bartender if he can place the beers in a bag, and he obliges. We all tip him well.

* * * *

As we walk out to the parking lot I get that depressed feeling when a good weekend is coming to a close. You always want to stay for more, extend it another day. But I have to get back to San Diego, back to work. It's depressing. I wish I had the money to do this indefinitely. I wonder how long I could last, doing this all day, every day. Maybe what they say about 'too much of a good thing' and all of that is true, but I don't buy it sometimes. I could handle it. If I have worries, I put them aside them when I am down here. Here, it's a good time with friends. You can't ask for more. At least, I can't. I'll take good friends over an expensive car any day. My family is always inquiring on where I blow all of my money. I haven't saved a dime, I don't drive a nice car, and I don't waste my money on expensive clothes. Sometimes I ask myself, "Where *does* all my money go?" As accurate as I can tell, I spend it on social activities. I never eat at home. I always drink. That's expensive. I'm always out and about. I actually do budget my money, and I know exactly where I spend it. Most people might not consider it a productive way of living my life, but there it is. I enjoy it. Good friends are like a relationship, or a marriage. You need to cultivate them, maintain them. That costs money. Money well spent, in my opinion.

In the car Ricardo informs us that he wants to come back down in a month or two. So does Israel. Israel, in particular, is enjoying himself. He loves weekends like this. So do I. They want commitments, however, for another trip down here. I have different plans. Then Israel suggests an alternative. Las Vegas.

"You know, we should go to Vegas later on this month."

"No, Vegas isn't my scene anymore," I tell him. "It used to be, but now it's filled with theme hotels, buffets, family fun, and everything else they can shuck at you."

"Come on, man. It'll be fun."

"No. I usually go down to Baja anyway. I want to get some fishing in. I'll go down there with you."

"No. I don't like Baja. There's nobody there. There's nothing to do."

And there's the general attitude that pervades Baja. Luxury isn't handed to you down there. You have to work at it to have fun. It's a different atmosphere down there. Not everybody enjoys it. I do.

"I need people around," Israel states.

"Oh, there's people down there," I tell him. "And there is plenty to do. There's this place called Mulegé, and it has everything. Empty white-sand beaches, good snorkeling, kayaking, fishing, you name it. It's also dirt cheap. And when I say deserted beaches, I mean it. I've spent days on those beaches down there and you might run into a few people. That's it."

"I want to relax when I'm on vacation, you know, be pampered," Israel says.

"I don't," I reply. "I want to do things I don't normally get to do."

"I agree with Evan," Ricardo says. "I would be interested."

"Get away from Southern California, I say."

"Vegas isn't Southern California," Israel retorts.

"Yeah, but it's organized fun. Sure, I enjoy playing the tables a bit, but I'm not going to spend a weekend in the desert to play a little blackjack. I was done with Vegas a few years ago. Too many Americans. Americans don't know how to have fun. They're stuck in their mindless rut, then go berserk at the first sign of a holiday weekend." I continue. "They're too loud. They're annoying. You can feel their frustration with their lives when they get drunk. You can tell they can't stand themselves. Or, the opposite, they're too cocky. Half the guys there I want to put my foot in their face. I'm not interested in partying with housewives and stuck up morons."

"Oh, there's a lot more there than housewives," Israel answers back, "and anyway, housewives without their husbands are ready for any excitement that comes their way."

There was a grain of truth in that. The frustrated wife is easy prey for any single guy looking for a little piece on the side. It's the organized fun that frustrates me.

"C'mon, Evan, Vegas isn't that bad."

"Ok, maybe it's not all bad. But for my time and money, I'd rather head south to Baja. If you guys want to do that, I'll set it up. I have all the connections down there. I know where to go. Like I said, we can go to Mulegé, or this other place called Loreto. Loreto is a bit larger; it's a sleepy fishing village, with a small American community of ex-patriots. Or, we can go all the way down to La Paz. The best fishing is down there. We can rent a boat and troll for marlin in La Paz."

"I've never been down there," Ricardo states.

"Neither have I," claims Eddie.

"See? Why not do something different. You want to drink? No problem, there's plenty of places. Snorkel? Scuba Dive? It's all there. Fishing? The best on the planet. And it's cheap. If you like it here, in Ensenada, you're going to love Baja."

I get some long faces, so I know I haven't convinced anyone. The only exception is Ricardo. They're still stuck on Las Vegas, but I dropped that scene. Vegas was great ten years ago, but it changed. It changed for the worse. The only advantage to Vegas now is they still let you drink on the street. You can walk down the strip with a drink in your hand without fear of reprisal. But I'm sure they'll take that away, too. They always do. The law enforcement braintrust of the United States must be losing sleep over the fact that in Las Vegas, a major American city, it is still legal to drink on the street. They'll put a stop to that. Watch. It must be driving them crazy. But the Casinos protect that one. Drunk gamblers lose more money. A drunk gambler is a good gambler. At least, in the Casino's eyes. So let them have their drinks, they say. But watch. Drinking on the street will disappear as well. Too many rule-crazy cops losing their minds over that one. Drinking on the street is Un-American.

Actually, The Strip in Las Vegas might constitute a 'tolerance zone', one of the last in the United States. A 'tolerance zone' goes against the grain of American Society. Nobody, or no thing, is above the law. Drinking on the street will be eliminated in Vegas. It's only a matter of time.

"C'mon Evan, Vegas."

"No, Baja."

"Ok. I guess I can do San Felipe," Ricardo says.

"No, San Felipe is not Baja. Mulegé is Baja. We have to go down *there*."

"It's the same—"

"—no it's not."

"Alright, you do your thing."

"I will, baby!"

"But we should come back down here."

"Definitely. Ensenada is always worth the trip."

XII

I wake up early in the morning, walk over to the local liquor store to grab a newspaper and a coffee, and walk back to my house. Mornings in San Diego always come with a blanket of fog. It's that perpetual marine layer again, but the sun will break through in an hour or two. It's the biggest mystery surrounding weather in Southern California: when is the sun is going to break through the mist. That's how mornings go in Southern California. I don't have to report in to work until eight this evening, so I have to whole day to myself. Gaby is down in Tijuana today, so I don't have to worry about that. Most of my friends are at work or school. I decide to make a trip to the mall in East Ridge. I'm bored enough. Maybe I can get in some shopping. I certainly could use some new clothes. You have to prioritize how you spend your money, and when you are constantly out and about all over town trivial items such as fine clothes get put on the wayside. Gaby always complains about my clothes. I'm the kind of guy that will wear the same pair of jeans for a few days straight. She hates it. So, it's off to the mall for me, but I don't know if I'm up to it. An American mall is an unhealthy culture shock when you have been spending most of your time in the underbelly of Tijuana.

The mall is a typical indoor shopping center. You enter, and your senses are assaulted by the same chain stores you can encounter in any mall in the United States. The stores might have different names, but they all sell the same thing. People walk around with their heads in their cell phones, speaking or texting some unknown person on the other side of the city. Or they have earphones plugged into their ears, cranking up the music as high as it can go without causing permanent damage to the eardrums. The effect is simple, but profound. Their reality is in their technology, not what's around them. They walk around like zombies, but alert zombies. The only thing that captures their attention is the new piece of technology right in front of them. To me, it's a big prison, and they are all locked in. They just don't know it yet. I wonder how it feels to be trapped in your own mind, with your gadgets acting as prison guards. All of their attention is focused on their gadgets. I'm curious to see whether I could stroll down a mall in my boxer shorts and provoke a reaction. I doubt it. I could probably make a roundtrip through the mall before somebody noticed I was walking around in my underwear.

The only people that might notice my attire are the mall employees that are paid to sell cell phones. They are loud, obnoxious, and aggressive. However, they have to be loud and obnoxious if they are going to get anybody's attention. It's almost impossible. As I walk by, they shout out to me, trying to grab my attention. I'm reminded of the strip club employees on La Revu, trying to lure me into a strip club. Here, they are trying to lure me into their booth and sell me a cellphone. Different products, but the same technique. I'm waiting for one of them to 'hook' my shirt sleeve. They don't, but they get close. I'm not going to purchase a cell phone. I refuse to get plugged in. It's one of the areas that Gaby and I agree on.

I walk into a store—I don't know which one—but it sells designer jeans and t-shirts. I would like a nice pair of jeans. Levi's are one of the greatest inventions of man. They work for any occasion. But I take one scan of the prices and I move on. I'm not paying that much for pants, even if they have a fancy name.

I walk into another store, and it seems more affordable. A girl walks up and asks if I need help, but then her pants start vibrating. She reaches in, grabs her phone, and walks off to have her conversation. Fine. I don't enjoy being pestered when I shop, anyway. I find what I'm looking for, make my purchase, and walk over to the 'food court.' Every mall in America has a 'food court.' The food is overprocessed, but edible. I look for something that appeals to me, order, and sit down to enjoy a meal by myself. The mall itself is immaculate. Everything is polished, shined, waxed, and cleaned. It's extremely sterile. Most hospitals aren't this clean. The 'food court' is cavernous, and the sounds of conversation echo and bounce around everywhere. You can hear the laughter bounce off the walls, clear the ceiling and the skylights, and travel up into the rafters. I try to make eye contact with somebody, anybody, but no. You won't get a 'hello' from a random stranger in here. It's not part of American etiquette in Southern California. I finish my sandwich, grab my bag, and go off to find a shoe store. There are many shoe stores in this mall, but to my surprise I find that they all sell the same shoes. Then I shop around for a new pair of sunglasses. There are about four different sunglass booths, but they all sell the same brands. I try to see if they have different prices, but the prices are the same. I make my choice, finish the transaction, then continue my stroll. I find the restroom, and enter. It's the cleanest public restroom I have ever seen. It's so clean, I feel like I have violated it by relieving myself. The urinal itself is spotless. It appears to have never been used. I wash my hands by waving my hand in front of the motion sensor on top of the water spigot. It releases a set amount of water, then automatically turns off, whether I am finished or not. If I want more water, I must wave my hand in front of it again. Then I wave my hand in front of the paper towel dispenser and it dispenses a specific amount of paper towel. Very efficient. The entire bathroom is a model of efficiency. The urinal itself is a 'non-flush' variety, to conserve water. Somehow, the urinal knows when I am finished, something clicks inside, and a small amount of water trickles out of it. The water spigot will only run a small amount of water for you to wash your hands, then it will turn off automatically. The paper towel dispenser releases a required amount of paper towel, just enough to dry my hands and nothing else. I feel like a car in an assembly line, with everything around me automatized to perform a job, at which point I need to move on to the next station. I wait for an invisible hand to push me out of the restroom when I finish, but they haven't invented it yet. I walk out at my own leisure.

Then I look for a music store. I walk up to one of the employees at the cell phone booth. They're the only ones in the mall I feel comfortable approaching. I ask one of them where the music store is at. He replies, "What music store? What's a music store? You can't buy music in here. But you can purchase this phone and download all the music you want." There is no music store in this mall. They don't exist anymore. Nobody buys cd's and records now. They download everything from their home computers. There are no music stores in this mall. I remember there used to be at least two. Not anymore. They have disappeared—for good. I love music stores. I would walk into a music store with no idea what I was going to purchase, but I would always come out with a good cd or two that I was excited about. Not anymore. No music stores, as far as I can see. They are relics. They have been replaced by cell phone stores. Very well. Everybody in the mall seems to be in a rush. Maybe they are getting their shopping in during their lunch break. It seems that way. I wonder if I tripped somebody? Probably nothing. They would get up, dust themselves off, and continue on. I would probably have to punch somebody in the face to provoke a reaction. I'm not up for assault charges, so I leave. Good riddance, until I need something else.

I go home, take a nap, wake up, eat dinner, and go to work. I don't want to work, but I need to. The drive up to downtown San Diego is nice. All the traffic at this hour is going in the opposite direction. I see all the drones in the south-bound lanes stuck in traffic as I cruise by in the north-bound lanes. 'Morons', I think to myself. I refuse to get stuck in a commute. I won't play along. I'm not a tool. At least my job provides that. The unusual hours work to my advantage; Generally, I can avoid the commuter traffic. I wouldn't do it at all, but I need to. I need money to spend in Tijuana. Life can get pretty boring if you are broke.

One day in a San Diego strip mall is enough for me to confirm all my worst suspicions. I don't worry, though. I have bigger fish to fry. Life is waiting for me on the other side of the border, and I have to be ready for it. I just have to manage my finances right, and enjoy time south of the border. The Palenque is coming up, and I have to plan around that. It's a big event for me; it always is.

Part II

XIII

The Palenque is an unusual event, and unique to Mexico. Despite what people think, Mexicans aren't normally dancers, but they are singers. The Palenque embodies that characteristic. Mexicans also enjoy drunken revelry, and the Palenque fills that need as well. It is situated in towns across Mexico; in Tijuana it celebrates the Dia de la Independencia. It is also the last place in Tijuana to hold legal cock-fights. The cock-fight is 'grandfathered' in, despite it being outlawed years ago in the rest of Tijuana. There are plenty of illegal ones, but this is the last place you can find a legal cock-fight.

The Palenque actually consists of a larger Feria, the Feria de Tijuana. The Palenque is just one of the venues; sometimes there is a sister venue, with much tamer shows. The Palenque is always the main event. There is also a large carnival that surrounds the Palenque. It is typical of a county fair that you can find in the United States, just less expensive and more diverse. It is best at night, and it has all the rides, games and places to eat and drink that you need. It also has a down-to-earth barnyard atmosphere that I enjoy. As my friend once said, it's a party for the 'Pueblo.'

Gaby and I show up early, so we can cruise around the fair a little bit before we make our way to the main stage. This year, the Feria is located in Hipódromo de Agua Caliente. Boulevard Agua Caliente is one of the main arteries of Tijuana; it starts in the Zona Rio and runs west through the rest of central Tijuana. It is also where the famous 'Caliente' racetrack is located. The whole area is referred to as 'Agua Caliente.' We park in the lot right next to the racetrack, then make our way over to the tented areas. The entire racetrack area is crammed with cars and people, with a few parties going on in the parking lot. Gaby and I enjoy the walk through the parking lot. We have a conversation about school, and her friends from school who might come down. They have never been to Tijuana before. We laugh at this. Imagine, living in San Diego and never having visited Tijuana. It's like shutting out half of the city. Gaby laughs at this. We agree that it is a calamity for all San Diegans who have never been down here. They must be scared, she thinks. They don't want to make the border line, I reply. That's a lame excuse, she tells me. They're lame for not coming down here, I argue. She retorts that she doesn't want to argue with me, because she agrees with me. We both laugh. Why are we arguing? We don't know. People look at us as we walk by. I look at Gaby, and I know why. She is wearing black pants, extremely tight. Her black shirt is also tight, and it doesn't leave a lot to the imagination. She wears a red scarf over the shirt, which sits in stark contrast to her black body-suit. Her hair is also jet black, long, and sweeps over her back. Her milky complexion sets it all off. She looks like a Spanish Señorita. Her hair is black, and her eyes are big and warm. It feels right to be walking next to her.

We walk up to the racetrack, and through the Caliente Zoo. There are a couple of bears, a few exotic birds, an ostrich, a lynx, a small panther, and a few other assorted wildlife. All the animals are lying down, and a few of them spare us a glance as we walk by. We look at the sad animals, trapped in their small cages, and we agree that we should do them a favor by letting them go. I get a little depressed observing the animals locked-up in their cages, so we agree to leave. I don't want to get depressed on a night like this. We make our way back to the lights of the Feria. It's exciting to walk through the parking lot, with so many people enjoying themselves. It's very similar to a tailgate in Kansas City. We walk up to the ticket booth and purchase our tickets to enter. The Feria is really designed to mimic an old fashioned County Fair, but with a Mexican flavor. We walk around, enjoying the sights, and I buy two tickets to ride on the Ferris Wheel. We grab our own cart, and as we wheel around we point out the Tijuana skyline as we reach the top each time. The border, lighted up at night, looks as if somebody took a knife and made an incision right through the city. San Diego and Tijuana should exist together, as one big city, but they're not. The border is an incision between them. It looks like a wound, but stitched up to stop the bleeding. That's what the border is: a wound right through the heart of the city. The breeze feels just right when you reach the top of the Ferris Wheel. When our ride is over, we find a place to eat. We stop into a tented area designed to look like a barn, fresh with haystacks for chairs. I order a bowl of *pozole*, without tortillas on the side. Gaby asks if there are *sopes*. They say no, they don't have any *sopes* to serve. She orders a salad. She looks at my plate and shakes her head.

"Why are you eating so much?"

"Better now. I don't want to worry about food the rest of the night."

"That bowl is huge. I can't believe you're going to eat it all."

"Believe it. You should think about yourself. You're eating too light. Grab something, while we're here."

"No, I'm ok. I've never been a big eater. Not like you, with your enormous bowl of pozole."

"It will help later on tonight. I can drink more."

Gaby shakes her head at that one. "There you go, planning your dinner around how much you are going to drink. See, I knew it. I knew you weren't that hungry."

"Hey, I'm hungry."

"Actually, it's funny. I've never seen somebody enjoy a meal as much as you. It's a sacred rite when you sit down for a real dinner."

"It ought to be. Dinner is my psychic anchor," I explain to her. "I need to sit down and enjoy a big meal. Preferably, after eight o'clock. Also, I need to sit down for at least an hour. It's fine if it takes forty–five minutes for my food to arrive. The later, the better. I don't like fast food. Give me slow food." Gaby is laughing now. I continue my rant—I'm not finished yet. "I can have a few drinks before then. Don't worry about the rest of the night. That one hour can ground me. Put me in the right mind set."

"What about dessert?"

"Of course, dessert."

"Do you have enough room?"

"There's always enough room for something else," I continue. "Dessert? Bring it on."

"What about appetizers?"

Gaby is enjoying herself. I'm on a roll.

"Appetizers? Of course, appetizers. While I'm waiting for my slow food, I eat appetizers. None of that salad stuff, either. I refuse to eat rabbit food. I need something to whet my appetite."

"Evan, the big eater."

"Just dinner. Forget the rest of the meals. Who says breakfast is the most important meal of the day? Not me."

"Doctors say that. And nutritionists."

"What do they know? Nothing. Don't believe a word they say. Doctors are purveyors in other people's misery, and nutritionists are on the food producer's payroll."

"Wow, I didn't know you were so philosophical about dinner."

"You know, I try to get to the bottom of things."

We look at each other. I think to myself, it would be nice to do this every night. She would probably disagree. I can see her mind wandering someplace else.

"How about you get to the bottom of your career?"

Here we go. I knew it. I knew it wouldn't take long for her to get there. We were having a great night. God forbid that it last long.

"I've been thinking about that. I'm thinking about going back to school."

"I knew you would say that! Well, don't think. Do. Everybody says that."

"I know. What about you?"

"Well, I should finish in three semesters."

"Took you long enough."

"Look who's talking. Anyway, I'll end up supporting you. It should be the other way around."

"Don't get traditional on me. You always try that. You're only traditional when it works to your advantage."

"Ha! Of course. I'm a girl that gets her way—one way or another."

I think about what she said. She does seem to get her way. Gaby is great at working her angles. She's definitely an enabler, not a follower. However, I'm not worried about that. I'm still focused on what she told me about a minute ago.

"So, you're going to support me?"

"You need somebody."

"Ah, you need somebody to take care of you as well. Who's going to put up with you? You need somebody like me."

"There are plenty of guys out there who would love the opportunity. And maybe I'm *looking* for somebody to take care of me."

"No, you're not. You couldn't stand to be dependent on somebody else."

She stares at me for a second. "You're right."

We both finish our drinks. I order another drink, this time a rum and coke. If I'm eating, I need something sweet.

I can't eat a meal with whiskey, or scotch. Those drinks are a meal unto themselves. Gaby orders a water. I see my opening, so I take it.

"Well, what do you want between us?"

She looks at me. She knows that was a pointed question. Her eyes bore right into me. I ambushed her with that question. I take a big spoon of my pozole, ignoring her eyes, and dig into my soup. I pull out a bone and put it into a cup on the table. Then I put some more diced onion in my soup, as well as some chopped radishes. Then I squeeze some lime into it. I do this all in silence, and I take my time doing it. When I look up, Gaby is still looking at me. I stare back at her.

"Well?"

"I don't know. It depends on what you want."

"Oh, nice one. Nice side-step."

"Nice ambush."

"Actually, I was just thinking that."

"See at least we are on the same page...sometimes. It helps."

"So, what are we going to do with each other?"

She looks at me again, weighing her response.

"Well...it depends on what you plan on doing. Now, and later. You work a little, but I need more than that. What are you going to do with yourself, Evan? It's good between us, but I need more. I always have a good time with you."

"I'm easy to get along with," I say.

"You think that, anyway."

"The truth is, I don't know what I'm looking for."

"Yeah, me neither."

"It's hard to know what you want. It always changes."

"And that's the problem."

"See, we're on the same page."

I pause, and look at her.

"Can we keep it exclusive?"

"You want that?"

I think about it, "Yes."

We walk out, back into the Feria, and she grabs my hand. That act, after our conversation, reassures me. It's weird how such a simple act can mean so much. Grabbing somebody's hand is simple; the message it implies is profound. It's comforting. She squeezes my hand. That must mean something else. It's those non-verbal, implicit messages that mean more to me. It didn't go that bad. For some reason, this date made me nervous tonight. I'm always nervous before I go out alone with Gaby. Our conversation, and everything that surrounded it, calms me down. Now, I feel like a drink. So does Gaby. If she's asking for a drink, it must mean everything is alright. We walk around to find a tent that serves alcohol. The Feria is packed now, and we fight a crowd as we walk down towards the Palenque arena.

We stroll around until we find another small bar, under a canopy that appears to be a relic from a nineteenth-century Russian circus. The canopy is out of place with the rest of the decorations of the Feria. I point at it and Gaby smiles. The place is empty. It only has a few tables in front of the bar. We sit down and the patronne seems happy to have a customer.

"What do you want?" I ask her.

"Martini. A dirty Martini."

"Well, if you want one of those, we better drink quickly. The crowd is getting big now."

"Let's find our friends first. They should be here by now."

"Alright, but drink first."

I signal the lady that we are ready to order.

"¿Qué va a ordenar?" she asks.

"A beer and a Martini," I inform her. "Can you make it dirty?"

"I can make them as dirty as you want them," the patronne replies in English.

Gaby smiles at her. "Not *too* dirty," she says.

"Extra dirty," I inform her.

"Wow, slow down," Gaby says. "The night hasn't started."

"Let's get it started."

"You know, you don't have to get drunk tonight. If you're looking to impress me, you don't have to."

"I know. But I want to tonight."

"You don't have to get drunk tonight. I'm just telling you. I have a better time with you when you're not."

"I'll try. But no promises."

"No, you can't make promises like that; I know."

"Why are you so bothered by it lately? You drink as much as I do."

"No, I don't. My cousins do, but I don't. It's just been tense lately between Sonia and myself. I don't like it."

"Why, what's the matter? Sonia is a big drinker. This should be the night of nights for her."

"I know, but lately she hasn't been herself. I don't know what's going on."

"Oh, I know what's going on."

"What?" She looks at me, "Adrian."

"Yep."

"What can we do?" Gaby asks me. "She's with him."

"There's nothing you can do. Deal with him, I guess. Live and let live."

"Evan, you're full of useless philosophy tonight."

"You know, I picked up a book awhile ago. A pretty big one. A ton of quotes in it. All kinds of useful stuff."

"When, last year?"

"Very funny. I'm sentimental tonight, that's all."

"Well, keep up the rhetoric. I enjoy it. I'll let you know if it's useful—or useless. But tell me, how do you justify, philosophically, your drinking?"

The patronne brings our drinks. I can see the olive juice swirling in Gaby's Martini. At least the she prepared it right.

"See this?" I ask Gaby, pointing to the beer in my hand. "This is *cervisia*. It's called a 'social lubricant.' You know what that means?"

"Yes, and I don't need a lesson in Latin from you," she tells me. "I told you I went to a private Catholic school down here. Latin is a requirement."

"Well, excuse me. I didn't take Latin in public school, but I pick up bits and pieces."

"I know, I've heard you. You do well for yourself."

She patted me on the knee.

"You know, you can be patronizing," I tell her.

"I try."

We finish our drinks and pay the bill. I take notice of the antique canopy, and it strikes me as out of place with the rest of the Feria. Despite the busyness of the Feria, we are the only ones under the canopy here. The legs of the canopy are made of polished wood, and appear to be many decades old. The canopy itself is tattered and dusty, but I can still see the red and orange hues under the dust. I can make out vague shapes, but nothing definite. The shapes on the canopy have faded over time. I wonder how old the canopy really is. A string of light-bulbs wraps around the tent. I inform the patronne that I enjoyed this place, especially the lighting and decorations. The martini was excellent Gaby informs her. She thanks me in Spanish, but with a strange accent. I wonder about that. Gaby and I walk arm-in-arm over to the center of the Feria, where all the action is, and we play a few games together. I'm buzzed enough now that the games are highly entertaining. We play the game with the ping-pong ball and the goldfish. Gaby actually manages to throw her ping-pong ball into a goldfish bowl, but we decline the prize. We can't carry around a plastic bag full of water and a gold-fish inside it. We walk around and observe the other booths. There's another one with a piece of string and a lighter. I enjoy the one with the golf balls. We both play the one with the metal rings and the bottle. Gaby always likes the game with the bee-bee gun. We finish, after wasting some money. I notice a *Caliente* booth and ask Gaby if I can place a few wagers on the baseball games tomorrow. She says 'no', because I'm going to do enough gambling tonight anyway. I agree with her. I notice now that a lot of the families have disappeared. It's older people now; adults. People our age, single and in pairs. Or in large groups, dressed up. Most of them are dressed to formally for a Carnival. Gaby and I are such people. I look at my watch.

"Well, shall we?"

"You know, I enjoy it more when it's just the two of us."

"Then why are you always looking for somebody else?"

"What? Who says I am?"

"You're always looking for somebody else. You always run off with another friend."

"I promise I won't run tonight. And it's not my fault I'm popular."

I stop walking at that.

"It must be nice to be popular. I'm surprised we didn't run into an old friend tonight."

"We haven't... yet." Her lips curl up into a smile. "Besides, I didn't know it bothered you that much. That's what I like about you. You're not jealous. So many guys are. Don't get jealous."

I feel bad about this.

"Sorry, I'm not. It shouldn't bother me."

"Don't let it bother you."

"I won't."

"Well, is it time?"

"Yes, let's head over."

We see the crowd of the Feria, and half of them are heading in our same direction. The rest are heading for the exits. I can feel the excitement. We approach the arena and everything is busy. People in line. People getting drinks before they get in line. People waiting to use the restroom. People trying to get past security. Gaby points out Eduardo

Tellez, waiting in line to use the bathroom. I look across and I see Sonia and Adrian at a table with Hector and Ricardo. They wave to us, and we wave back. They are all standing around a barrel that serves as a table, under the L.A. Cetto tent. All the tables are wine barrels. There are tents all around the arena, representing different vineyards, distilleries, and breweries. The tents are brightly colored; designed to grab your attention. All of the tents are labeled with their sponsors. Most of the crowd is filling in tables under the canopies. The tents are filled with lights, tables and chairs, smoke, waiters and waitresses running about, and people clamoring for an empty table. It's a rush to find a table. No problem for us; a table is already waiting with our friends standing around it. It's pleasant to have a table waiting for you, full of friends. Their tent is red. There are two bottles of wine at their table, almost finished. I'm surprised that Ricardo is drinking wine. He never drinks wine. Gaby and I walk up and I grab a glass. I fill it with the merlot, and swirl it around. I might as well look like I know what I'm doing. Somebody bumps into me from behind. It is getting crowded now. There are not enough chairs to go around. It's not a problem, but I don't want to spill my wine. Sure enough, I get bumped again and I have to grasp my wine glass with two hands as I walk around the table. I greet Sonia, Hector, and Ricardo, in that order. I finally greet Adrian. Hector shakes my hand. Ricardo slaps my back. Sonia gives me a kiss on the cheek. I say 'hi' to Adrian. Adrian nods. He greets Gaby with a kiss on the cheek, and then whispers something to her. I can't hear what. Gaby smiles. Gaby and Sonia stand next to each other. There is music; a Mariachi band is playing in the background. I look around, and everybody is standing and sitting and having a good time. I pour myself another glass of wine. I know I shouldn't be mixing alcohol like this, but I have no choice. The bottles are empty now, but Hector orders two more. They come, and the waitress uncorks the bottles for us. She pours a little into each glass. Gaby also has a glass. Eduardo returns from the bathroom, and he has to greet Gaby and myself. It is customary, but difficult in the crowd. The music from the Mariachi continues, but is partially drowned out by the crowd. Eduardo stands with me, and we talk. We are excited about the concert. He has never been to a Palenque, but has heard plenty about it. I try to convey the experience to him, but I finally give up under the influence of the wine. I tell him to be patient, he will find out for himself soon enough. Gaby tells me it is useless to describe it; you have to be there. We look at each other, and touch glasses.

"When should we head inside?"

"In a few minutes. When we finish these bottles."

I scan the crowd under the tent and notice that some people appear to be settling down around their table. Ricardo notices the same thing.

"What's going on?" Ricardo asks. "Isn't this thing about to start?"

"Some people don't go in for the cock-fights," Hector informs him. "They'll just wait out here and drink. Then they will go inside around eleven o'clock or so."

"Yeah, it's cheaper to drink outside than it is inside," I tell Ricardo.

I glance at the tables around us and it appears that about half of the people are finishing up. The other half still have full bottles and food in front of them.

"Only about half look like they are going inside for the cock-fight," I say.

"Yeah, that's about right," Hector answers. "It actually works out, because it's not that crowded for the fights."

Gaby weighs in on our conversation, "I wouldn't mind staying out here and waiting for Chente," she says. "It's nice out tonight. Why not stay out here for a while?"

"No, no, no," Ricardo says. "I want to see the fights."

"So do I," I say.

"Me too," Hector chimes in.

"C'mon Gaby, let's go inside," Sonia reassures her. "It's not that bad if we all chip in for bottles. I want to see the birds fight too."

Sonia seals the deal for Gaby. I nod at Sonia and raise my glass to her. She holds her glass and taps mine. Her brothers follow suit. Leave it to Sonia to *want* to see the cock-fight. Not many women are interested in that spectacle.

"Looks like it's going to be a good one," Sonia says.

"It always is, in Tijuana." Hector replies.

The Palenque was about to begin.

* * * *

The Arena that houses the Palenque is not large. It sits about six thousand people. The security is tight; it takes us a few minutes to get in. There is a large line. People in Tijuana are always waiting in lines. It is the nature of the city. The security is tight. It must be. There can be problems at a Palenque. I believe it is the sight of blood before the concert. The blood incites the crowd. The cock-fights precede the concert, and the singer is always a Mariachi or folk singer. The "Palenque" literally refers to the cock-pit, the dirt covered arena where the fighting-cocks tear each other to shreds. Afterwards, the Palenque singer uses the dirt-and-blood covered pit as a stage to sing. After a good evening in the cock-pit, you can still see blood on the dirt as the Mariachi come out. The cock-fights never start before eight o'clock in the evening; and the singer never begins his performance before eleven o'clock at night. There is no spectacle to compare it to in the United States. An event such as this does not exist. It could not exist. There are laws against it. The public has no stomach for it. A social event lasting until four o'clock in the morning is unheard of in the United States, but one year Rocio Dúrcal didn't even come out to perform until two o'clock in the morning. She was so high on cocaine, and the audience was so drunk after two hours of drinking scotch waiting for her to come out, that the show was a travesty. They finally had to drag her out of her hotel room, and when she finally arrived Rocio only sang for an hour and a half. She had a hard time standing. Even then, nobody got out of the arena until the other roosters were crowing. After that evening, Rocio Dúrcal entered Tijuana legend as one the greatest Palenque singers to perform here. The people of Tijuana consider a spectacle such as that the pinnacle of showmanship.

"Evan, how does this work? I've never been to a cock-fight before," Eddie asks me.

The crowd was milling into their seats. We were sitting in the first row of the second level. The Palenque Arena is broken down into two main sections, surrounding the cock-pit. The first level goes up about twenty rows, then a ridge up to the second section. We were on the first row of the second section, with a perfect view of the stage.

"I like these seats the best. You have an unobstructed view of everything, and you don't want to be down there in the first section anyway. Too much trouble."

"Why?" Eddie asks.

"That's where all the drug-traffickers and their kids are. That's where all the fights start."

"Ok."

"Anyway, it's cock-fight first, music second. There will be a few fights, then they will clear the cock-pit and let the band in. Vicente Fernandez usually doesn't get started until midnight. It's a good two to three hours of cock fights, then a good three hours of singing. Maybe more."

Eduardo and I were standing up, leaning against the railing. We watched as the pit attendants cleaned the arena and set up equipment for the show tonight. All the gambling paraphernalia was being arranged.

"How do you bet?"

I look at him.

"You can bet with the house, or you can make side bets with anybody around here. Bets made with other people get paid immediately, and be careful. It's your word. If you want to bet with the house—and it's safer—they throw these little white balls all around. Just grab one, open it up, bet your color, put your money in, and throw it back. They will throw your slip back up, and you're ready to go. If you win, just let them know. They'll come and pay you out."

"Weird."

"Yeah, but this happens only here. It's easier to bet with other people, just make sure you can cover it. It can get nasty real quick if you can't."

"Ok."

"Yeah, just keep it to twenty dollars at a time or something. Don't get crazy."

The Palenque was only half-full for the beginning of the cock-fights. The rest of the crowd will make their way in gradually as the fights go on. All kinds of denizens of Tijuana, young and old, are here for the show. People are mingling about everywhere, finding their seats and trying to get the attention of a hostess to purchase drinks. There are attendants down on the cock-pit, waiting to take bets. There are also some officials, speaking with the owners of the roosters, and checking on the general fitness of the birds. The birds are kept in cages until their time comes. All the movement has the quality of a good boxing match, a prize fight waiting to happen. Everybody down there in the pit is walking around in a big damn hurry, trying to look important. I wave my hand to catch the attention of an attendant. I send a bet down to the galley. I'm going "green." Basically, there are two farms providing the cocks. They also compete against each other. There is "green," and "blue." They showcase their birds before the match, much like in horse-racing, and you can view and evaluate each of the cocks that are prepared to fight that evening. They treat it like horse-racing, where you can appraise the horses before they race. They try to make a science out of it. Maybe there is a science to evaluating horses by sight, but they apply it to cocks as well. Many enthusiasts like to do this; they think it gives them an edge in their wagering. I disagree. When those cocks go at it, I think it comes down to the temperament of the bird and dumb luck. I wave my hand and an attendant throws a white ball in my direction. I open it up, mark 'green', place two hundred pesos inside, and throw it back down to him. The attendant takes the money, marks my slip, and throws it back up to me.

I lean back over to Eduardo. "Ok, ready? Here they come."

The cock handler's hold their birds like a beloved pet, cradling them, stroking them lovingly. I don't know if they do that to calm them down, but it's damn bizarre, considering they are about to let those birds loose to engage in mortal combat. Maybe they finally have a hint of remorse for what they are about to do. It's hypocritical to show compassion now. Those bird handlers should have showed compassion yesterday, when it counted, and let the locks on those cages go.

The birds themselves are big, with razor-sharp spurs on each foot. One year an owner almost lost his life to one of those spurs. He was handling his cock and the bird attempted to escape his hold, slashing to owner in the process. He took a cock-spur to the arm, slashing an artery. He almost bled out. Occupational hazards.

"They have ranches, or what?" Eddie asks.

"Sure, you can raise them anywhere. Supposedly the

best ranches are actually in the United States, but I don't know. Just ask one of them after the fight. If they are from the U.S., they will probably be low key. It's highly illegal up in the States."

"Do they have rounds, like in boxing?"

"No, of course not," I tell him. "They go at it until one of them gets killed. It usually doesn't take that long."

"Can you check them out before a fight?"

"Yes, but I never bothered with that. It's not like horse racing. At least, not to me. I can't tell a good one from a bad one."

Ricardo has been listening in, and looks over at Eduardo.

"You sure you're going to be ok.?" Ricardo asks him.

"Yeah, I think so," Eduardo says.

"Don't worry, both Gaby and Sonia have come before, and they handle it fine," I tell him. "Americans aren't used to this, though. Any competition that has blood is Un-American."

"Ha. Yeah, no more blood sports in the U.S."

"Nope. And it's disappearing down here as well. This is it for legal cock-fights in Mexico. They only happen in Palenques now."

"They still have illegal ones in Tijuana?"

"Oh, of course," I tell him. "Your uncle used to raise fighting-cocks."

"Really?"

I turn to Gaby, who was deep in conversation with Sonia.

"Gaby, what Uncle used to raise fighting-cocks?" I ask her. "What was his name?"

"My Tio Armando. I haven't seen him in years." Gaby turns her attention back to Sonia.

"Yeah, it was Tio Armando," Ricardo says. "I remember the cages he used to keep them in."

"He kept them in cages?" I ask.

"Yeah," Ricardo replies. "You have to keep them separated, obviously. That guy used to raise all kinds of animals." "Where is he?" I ask. "What happened to him?"

"Nothing. My Tio Armando is a *man apart*. That guy would disappear for weeks at a time on fishing trips down to Baja and come back with coolers full of fish. He would go all by himself. He never stays anywhere for too long. But he has the knowledge. He can tell you how to make barbacoa in the ground. He knows how to make *birria de chivo*."

"You make birria out of a goat?" I ask.

"Yes, real birria is called *birria de chivo*. Goat-birria," Ricardo informs me.

"I remember that," Eddie says, "it tastes real strong. They also can make it out of chicken. That tastes better."

"I remember the real stuff though," Ricardo continues, "they would drive out to the ranches outside Tijuana and buy a goat. My uncles kept it tied up at their house for a few days. Then they would slit the goat's throat, hang it upside-down to drain the blood, butcher it up, throw it in a stew, and a few hours later everyone is eating birria."

Eduardo shakes his head.

"It was a big family party," Ricardo continued. "Even Sonia and Gaby were there, but they were pretty small. I doubt they remember it."

"Yeah, nobody has seen my Uncle in years. Who

knows if he does it anymore," Eduardo informs me.

"Did you ever to go one of his cock-fights?" I ask Ricardo.

"No, I was too young. They wouldn't have taken a kid. I do remember that goat, though. It did this small little scream when they cut its throat. The birria tasted pretty good."

"So there's no more cock-fights on the streets?" Eduardo asks. "I'm sure there are," Ricardo tells his brother. "But I don't know where. If we ever see our Tio Armando again, we can ask him."

"*If* we see him again."

"Anyway, there's a lot of shenanigans in underground fights," I inform Eduardo.

"What, they drug them or something?"

"Probably, but it really has to do with those spurs the birds have. They have to be a certain length, and they can put chemicals on them."

"Chemicals?"

"Yeah, chemicals to drug the other bird. They'll put it on the blade, so when the other bird gets cut, it will get drugged. That's illegal though, even here."

"But not on the street?"

"They can't regulate on the street."

"And they regulate it here?"

"I guess. This is as close to legitimate as you can get."

The attitude of the crowd changes, and I know something is about to happen. Some people stand up, others sit down. You can feel the change in the crowd because the fight is about to begin. The first two roosters are released into the cock pit, and they immediately start circling each other. The first couple rows start hooting and hollering, but I'm suspicious about that. I doubt the birds care if they are being egged-on. Then the wings start flapping, the feathers start flying, and the blood starts running. My green bird catches the other on the side with a well placed spur, forcing him to limp. The hurt bird doesn't care, and tries to get leverage by flapping his wings. He manages to get on top of the green bird. He kicks hard and catches green bird in the face. The spur was well placed, and now green bird is blind in one eye. I'm worried about that, thinking that I'm going to lose my two-hundred pesos. There's plenty of blood now, and it can't be much longer. Those birds only have so much blood in them. Instead of backing off due to the eye, my green bird goes on the offensive and starts slashing with his cock-spur, alternating between left and right. Blue bird tries to back off, but too late. The green bird keeps kicking until the blue bird keels over. The fight is over. My green bird won, with one eye and everything.

White plastic balls fly all over the arena and money exchanges hands by majority of the crowd. I collect a white ball, place my slip in it, and throw it down to a ring attendant. He catches it, opens the ball and glances at the slip, stuffs a few bills in it, and throws it back to me. A straight and easy exchange. No hassles here. Our bottle of Scotch finally arrives, and the waitress gives us cups and a bottle of mineral water. I look at the bottle—Buchanan's Twelve—open it up, and take a sip directly from the bottle. Gaby smacks my shoulder as I do it. I pass the cups all around, and mix my scotch and water. I try to explain the intricacies of the cock-pit, but they are lost on Eduardo and Ricardo. They are not interested, except which bird won. Ricardo is much more interested in what there is to drink. Adrian leans over and hands him a cup.

"Why scotch?"

"Why not."

"Hey, Adrian, take it easy," I yell, "no trouble tonight!" I look across to Adrian, and he shoots me a dirty look. That guy can't handle his liquor for shit.

"Whatever, Evan. You just take care of yourself."

"Hey, it's a long night. You might want to sip that, that's all."

"Fuck off."

Gaby grabs me, "Hey, quit giving him trouble. That's the last thing we need tonight."

"That guy brings trouble everywhere he goes."

I have had a few drinks before I got here, with Gaby, so I'm drunk enough to be careless. But I don't care. I'm tired of everybody kissing his ass just because he is with Sonia. I respect Sonia, but that guy is ridiculous.

"I'm not going to look for trouble," I tell Gaby.

"You already are."

Hector looks annoyed at me. "The next birds are coming out. You might want to make your bet now. You won last time, didn't you?"

"Yep. Time to double up!"

"Going Green again?"

"Green is lucky tonight."

The Blue birds win the next three fights.

The scotch is good; Buchanan's Twelve, and with the mineral water it goes down smooth. The number twelve refers to the number of years the scotch has been aged. The larger the number, the longer the scotch has been aged, and the smoother it is. It also corresponds to price. Everybody is in rare form tonight; Sonia is having fun, despite her handicap. Gaby is laughing hard at one of her cousin's jokes, and I feel good despite losing most of my money.

"Hey, Evan, how much are you down?"

I look over at Adrian.

"Don't worry about it. Green will come back."

"Blue is the way to go tonight," he tells me. "You want me to buy you a beer?"

"I'm fine."

Gaby pulls my shirt again, "Why is he trying to buy you a beer when we have a bottle right here?"

"He's not trying to buy me a beer. He's baiting me, that's all."

"Ignore him."

"I can't. He's drunk."

"Yes, and so are you."

I try to grab an attendant's attention to place another bet, but Adrian calls over, "Evan, twenty right here. I'll take Blue."

Gaby whispers in my ear, "Don't."

"Twenty."

"Alright."

"Oh my god," Gaby looks up in the air.

The birds are released, and the green one looks timid. He doesn't want to fight. He begins to circle around the cock-pit, and finally one of the handlers has to push him in the direction of the other cock. They begin their duel, but at a serious disadvantage for my bird.

"Ah, Evan, looks like you picked the wrong one again. That happens often."

Gaby looks over, "What's that supposed to mean?"

Sonia grabs Adrian and whispers something to him. I look back down and see my green bird on the floor.

"Blue again! Don't worry, Evan, it was a fun bet anyway. I'm not going to collect from you."

"What? Here." I flip my twenty dollar bill on the ground.

"Pick that up."

"You."

I leave the bill on the ground, and Gaby finally picks it up. She stuffs it in her pocket. I sit there for a few minutes, brooding. I want my twenty dollars back, but I'm not going to ask Gaby for it. It would be bad taste. I know she's doing it on purpose. I'll just ask her to buy me something later.

Two more birds are released, and they begin their duel. This time, both animals look strong, and prepared to fight. It's another flurry of feathers and blood before the green bird comes out of it victorious. The Green Bird's win emboldens me. Finally, I feel my luck changing. I feel a tug on my shoulder, and it's a middle-aged woman, looking to make a bet.

"Quiero Azul. I want Blue. Do you speak Spanish?" she asks.

"Yes, I speak Spanish. You want Blue? Alright. ¿Cuanto?"

"Quinientos pesos."

"No, trescientos."

She stares at me for a moment, trying to shame me into a larger bet, but I stick to my golden rule of twenty dollars at a time.

"Ok, trescientos."

I nod at her. Three hundred pesos is close enough to twenty bucks.

Gaby looks at me, "Be careful taking side bets. Do you still have cash?"

"Yes, of course. I'm not going to make a bet I can't cover."

"Alright, but try to stick with the house. It's safer."

"I'm not here to play it safe."

"That's a dangerous attitude, especially here. And I don't like it when you bet when you're drunk."

"When I asked you out the first time I was drunk," I tell her. "That wasn't exactly a safe bet. Did it pay off?"

"Ha! Let's wait and see."

"Yeah, I'm still waiting for the payoff."

"Really? So am I."

I look at her, but there's a smile on her face. She's baiting me. Gaby doesn't like to gamble, which is too bad. She would be a great gambler. She's always hedging her bets, with everything and everybody, including me.

"Are you hedging your bet with me?"

She laughs at that one. "Always."

"Should I keep going green?"

"No, and that's your problem. You always bet with emotion. You're too attached to the green birds."

"It's called loyalty. I'm loyal to the green birds."

"Loyalty is fine, and it has its points, but it might not be successful. Loyalty will only take you so far," instructs

Gaby. "The blue birds look stronger. They're definitely more aggressive. If I were you I'd start betting 'blue.'"

"Watch, green will come through yet."

The blue bird wins again. I hear Adrian yelling at me, but I'm busy pouring myself another cup of Scotch. I hate losing bets, but losing them in front of Gaby and Adrian is worse.

"Evan, green keeps going down!" Adrian again. "Here, let me buy you a beer."

"I don't need a beer—"

"—I think you do."

Gaby grabs me, "I'm going to the bathroom before Vicente comes out. Come with me."

It is and isn't a request.

"Your woman calls," Adrian yells at me.

"Ignore him." Gaby leads me out by the hand.

We walk the other way down the aisle, and back to the bathrooms. It's getting hot, and the crowd is picking up energy. I look down and I see the pit crews raking the cockpit, trying to cover the blood with the dirt. Vicente Fernandez will be ready soon.

"Don't let him get to you," Gaby tells me. "And you already have had too much to drink. I want you to stop."

"What? I've only had a few drinks."

"Yeah, and a few before we got here. I don't know why you had to drink before we arrived. As if there wasn't going to be enough to drink."

"Hey, just trying to get the party started a little early, that's all."

"Vicente is going to be out there for about three hours. Just remember that. And I want to sing and enjoy myself with my family, not babysit you."

"You're not going to babysit me."

Hector comes up beside us.

"Israel and Susana just got here."

"Missing all the fun, of course," I say.

"Can we put them between us and Adrian?" Gaby asks Hector.

"Yes."

"Hector, you don't need to play Godfather here."

"I bought these tickets, so save it."

"It's true. You're the family benefactor. If there's any trouble, call Hector."

"I'm getting tired of it."

"No, you're not. You like it. Every family needs one."

I put my arm around his shoulder. "Besides, you haven't had a drink yet." My speech sounds slurry to me. "Why aren't you drinking?"

"The night is young, Evan, don't you worry. And you sound like you've had enough to drink for both of us." He winks at me and pats my stomach.

"Thanks."

Hector walks back down to our seats. I don't worry too much about him. Hector is a first rate drinker. He can be drunk in an hour. Hector rarely messes with the small stuff. He's not a big beer or wine guy. Hector goes straight for the hard stuff. Tequila, Scotch, Vodka. He will take double shots, one after another. I never try to keep up with Hector; nobody does. The only problem with that, he taps out quickly. He has a reputation among everybody. The expression is 'Calienta Huevos.' In English, it is 'Hot Balls.' It means he gets everybody fired up to go out, to party. Then when the time comes, he crashes out. Now, I never believed he had true 'Calienta Huevos.' What I think it really is—he just started the party too early. Hector would get everybody fired up to go out, then start drinking around eight o'clock. By ten–eleven o'clock, he was finished. That's when everybody else was ready to hit the town. Hence, his reputation of having 'Calienta Huevos' was born. I don't think he was a true 'Hot Balls' person however; he just started drinking too early. But in terms of capacity of empathy, nobody has more. Nobody gives more to the family than Hector. I respect him for it.

"You're lucky to have a cousin like Hector," I tell Gaby.

"Our whole family is."

"He is the Godfather. The family benefactor."

"Where is his girlfriend, anyway?"

"I don't know. I think they got into a fight. I saw Hector tearing up some pictures earlier."

"What? Of him and Amanda?"

"No, some pictures of her and some other guy."

"Uh, oh."

"Yeah, and all of a sudden Amanda is heading down to Guadalajara to visit family?"

"Really? What about her house?"

"Hector is going to house sit."

"That's where the after-party will be."

"There's no after party on a night like this. We might not get out until three, four in the morning."

"True."

Gaby finally reaches the bathroom, and I wait for her. I can hear the trumpets and guitars now. People start to run to their seats. A couple of drunks get pushed to the floor, and they have a hard time getting up. People are rushing to their seats, and they might get trampled. They are also drunk. It is much too early to be that drunk. They are not going to make it, unless they have somebody looking out for them. I look around, and they appear to be alone. I don't want to see them get hurt. I run over there to help them up. I have to push some people out of the way, and I grab the first guy and throw him up. The second guy gets up on his own and they run off to their seats. They don't even thank me. Fine, whatever. I go back to the bathroom, waiting for Gaby. Typical Gaby, as soon as the show starts she needs to use the restroom. Gaby comes walking out and grabs me by the arm.

"Let's go!"

We walk back, and see Israel with Susana in our seats. Israel is standing up, hands cupped to his mouth, shouting down at Vicente Fernandez. Suzie is sitting down, looking very polite. I stand next to Israel. He finally notices me, and we embrace.

"Where the hell have you been?" I shout at him.

"Oh, we just got here," he shouts back. "We were out at the fair. Then we ate a late dinner. I wanted some food in my stomach before we got here." Gaby shoots me a look. "I don't think Susana would appreciate the cock-fight," Israel tells me.

The lights dim around the arena. Vicente Fernandez motions to his Mariachi, lined up around the cock-pit, and they begin playing their instruments. Vicente holds up his microphone, and a single spot-light beams down on him, blotting out the rest of his band. Now, it's only Chente standing in the middle of the ring, his costume glittering in the light, the blood and dirt mingled in underneath his feet. All eyes are on him.

Susana waves at Gaby as Vicente begins to sing. Everybody is standing now, singing along. Our view is unobstructed; we can see the whole venue. All the attention is now focused on 'Chente'. After Vicente finishes his song, he walks over to the crowd and a young lady whispers something in his ear. He turns back and yells at his Mariachi. They begin the next song.

"Is he taking requests from the galley?"

"He always does. His shows are different every night."

"How do they know what to play?"

"His Mariachi know all of his songs. That's how he does it."

"That's why he's the best."

"That's why we all sing along. We know all the songs as well."

Gaby leans over, "He doesn't really write his own songs. It's his voice that matters. He could have been an Opera singer."

"What do you mean, he doesn't write his own songs?"

Israel chimes in, "He tried a few times, and his songs were horrible. The best writers write songs for him, and he sings them. Gaby is right; it's his voice that counts."

"He doesn't write his own stuff?"

"No. He's a singer. But you'll see. He will drop his mike pretty soon, and sing directly to the crowd. You can hear his voice all the way at the top. And his memory is tremendous; he remembers every song. That's why he can take requests like that. You can request anything, and they'll play it and he'll sing it. Even if he *is* drunk."

"Yeah, that's why he has a table in the cock-pit," Hector informs me. "That's a bottle of Tequila, not water. He drinks as the show goes on."

"Does he get drunk?"

"Oh yeah. If he gets drunk enough, he refuses to leave the stage. Eventually security will drag him off-stage, or they'll turn the lights on and cut his mike. I've seen him sing until four in the morning. Four hours, non-stop."

"I want to see that."

"Just keep an eye on how many shots he takes. That will be a good indication on how good the show will be."

The amazing part is the crowd participation. Vicente knows the songs, but so do the rest of the audience. We almost act as his chorus.

"Damn, some people are crying already," Ricardo quips.

"That's because he's singing *Puro Cachanilla*," Gaby tells him. "They love that song here."

"Yeah, it's directed to us."

Even Gaby is singing along, standing and swaying as she does it. I've never seen her like this before.

"Israel, what's a *Cachanilla*?"

"A flower. But it refers to somebody from Mexicali, or up here on the border. It's a flower that grows only up here in Northern Mexico."

"Yeah, that's why everybody sings it."

Adrian shouts over, "How come you don't know that, Evan? Damn, everybody knows that. Catch up, man."

"Shut up."

"C'mon man, sing along. Or can't you? Your woman is singing along, why don't you? Oh, you can't, because you don't know the song. Why come here if you don't know the songs?"

Sonia grabs Adrian and tells him to shut his face.

"No, I'm not going to shut my face. C'mon, Evan, sing. I want to hear you sing, that's all. Just one song. Gaby, how are you with a guy that doesn't know how to sing?"

Adrian is obnoxious when he's drunk, and he's been drinking for five hours straight now. Gaby shouts at him, "Don't worry, he'll learn them. Why don't you have another scotch? Here, I'll pour it for you."

She hands him another cup of Scotch and water. Adrian gives her a strange look.

"What did you do that for," I ask her.

"At this point, it's better for everybody if he passes out. The cops can take him away for all I care."

"Good point."

Gaby shouts back over to him, "Next song is yours Adrian, I want you to sing the whole song."

Adrian looks at her again.

"C'mon, sing. I want to hear you sing."

Adrian turns around and shuts up.

"See, Evan, that's how you handle a belligerent drunk," Gaby tells me. "Take notes."

"I'm taking them, and I don't need you to stand up for me."

"Anytime, anytime." She smiles at me and the game is over.

Gaby has that easy social grace, and she can handle any situation. She diffuses tension, and that's why I'm with her.

"You know, you can't handle every situation like that."

"Why not? He's jealous, that's all."

"Jealous of what? And if it comes down to blows, you can't solve it your way then."

"It won't come to that. Enjoy the show, it's one of a kind."

"Definitely."

"By the way, what happened to Sonia?"

Gaby leans over, but Sonia is nowhere to be found. Adrian notices us, and points up to the bathrooms. Convenient exit. I wonder if Sonia is coming back.

Vicente Fernandez is ramping up his act. He now sits at the table he placed in the cock-pit, and he sings directly to the bottle of Tequila. The only thing on the table is a bottle of Tequila, a jigger, and a couple of crumpled pieces of paper where he had taken requests for songs. This is an unusual ensemble of props: A table, a chair, a bottle of Tequila, and a jigger. He sits, alone at the table, with a single spotlight on him. He commences to sing to the bottle of Tequila. He treats the bottle of Tequila as a long-lost lover. The entire song, he is singing to the Tequila bottle. The whole crowd loves it. Everybody is hollering and cat-calling him. I respect a man who can sing to a bottle. Chente points to another member of the audience, a woman, and she runs onto the cock-pit and hands him another note, then gives him a quick kiss on the cheek. She runs back to her seat. Chente makes a big scene of opening the note, reading it, tipping his Sombrero to the lady, then walking back to his Mariachi so they know what song to play. It has all of the elements of staged drama, all for our amusement.

"You know that note has her phone number on it," said Ricardo.

Eduardo laughs, "Yeah, and her hotel and room number."

"Probably. This is a real act, though. It's crazy."

"See, Chente does this, but he didn't create it. A singer called Jose Alfredo Jimenez was the first to do this," Ricardo informs us.

"First to do what?"

"Sing to a bottle of Tequila—on stage."

"Are these his songs?"

"Oh, yeah," Ricardo says. "Most of the good old Ranchero songs were written by him, especially the drinking songs. He started all of that."

"And he sang to the bottle?"

"Yes. Vicente sings Jose Alfredo songs, just with a better voice."

"I want to sing to a bottle," I say.

"I'll give you one tonight," Ricardo tells me. "Then you can sing all you want."

"Don't encourage him," Gaby says.

"I don't sing," I tell them.

"I know. You're not Mexican. You can try, though. You're almost Mexican. You're also drunk, which is the secret ingredient."

"What happened to Jose Alfredo?"

"He passed away. He had a liver."

"I don't doubt it."

"His best album was called 'El Cantinero.'"

"What, the 'Barfly?' Well, that would explain the liver."

Sonia walks back down and goes back to her seat. I give her a glance, but she avoids any eye contact.

The waitress brings us another bottle, with cups and water. Hector pays, and gives her a tip.

"Thanks, Hector. I appreciate this."

"Anytime."

"You're the family benefactor."

"I try. I'm also the only one who works for a living. Just taking care of my brothers, sister, and cousins."

"He does," Ricardo says. "Let me take care of this bottle right now."

Ricardo grabs the bottle and pours himself a drink. Straight scotch. He doesn't bother to mix in the water. Gaby and Sonia exchange glances. Eddie gets a hold of the bottle and pours two drinks, one for myself. Hector then takes the bottle and keeps it for himself.

"Hector, you take care of everybody."

Sonia gets up and gives her brother a hug. Gaby follows suit.

"It's my treat." Hector has tears in his eyes. Out of everybody, he's the one that tries to keep the family together. This outing was his idea. It's always his idea.

I whisper to him, "What are you going to do about Adrian?"

He just nods his head. He knows, but they all try to ignore Adrian. They can't ignore him forever. I look over at Adrian, sitting alone, but he's too drunk to care. He is swaying in his seat with his cup in his hand. Adrian tries to sing the song, but can't catch up.

Vicente is standing up again, and the table is gone. That part of the act is over. Vicente addresses the crowd directly and informs us that as long as we want him to sing, he will sing. The crowd erupts at this.

"That means he's drunk," Hector states.

"Will he really sing as long as we keep up the applause?" I ask.

"No. Eventually, his band will grab him and take him away. Or they'll shut the show down. He'll keep it up for awhile though. He's drunk enough by now."

"How old is he?" I ask Hector.

"Oh, he's in his fifties, sixties by now. He started off by singing on buses in Tijuana."

"Really?"

Gaby chimes in, "Yeah, that story is famous. He would sing on buses making their routes all over Tijuana, and somebody riding the bus one time heard his voice and picked him up. That was back in the sixties, though."

"Damn, what a start."

Everybody is standing up, having a good time, except Susana. She is still in her seat. She seems to be waiting for something. I look up and I see Adrian also staring at her. He looks up and we make eye contact. He rolls his eyes. If there's one thing we have ever agreed upon, it's our mutual assessment of Susana. She adds nothing to the group. The problem is, she's not a bad person. She's not. But she adds nothing. She does nothing. She seems to be waiting for something, but I'll be damned if I can figure out what. I hope she's not waiting for Israel, because that might take awhile. I doubt Israel has any interest in settling down, or doing anything by the ordinary. I see her, sitting next to

Israel, but really by herself. I can't figure out why she keeps coming to these things.

"Suzie, what's up? Why don't you have a drink?" I ask her.

"You know I don't drink."

I lean over, behind Israel, who is still standing up and ignoring his date, and address Susana directly, "Why did you come here? Do you like Vicente Fernandez?"

"I don't really like him, but I'm worried about Israel. I don't want him to try to cross the border drunk."

"Oh, don't worry. We wouldn't let him do that. We have a house right here where everybody can pass out."

Gaby hears our snippet, "No, we can't use that house. Hector already said so."

"Suzie, don't worry about Israel. He can take care of himself."

Susana just stares at me. "Ignore him," Gaby says to Susana. "He's had too much to drink."

"No, I haven't."

Adrian, who has overheard our whole conversation, speaks up, "Yeah, Susana, relax. Let Israel drink. We know you don't drink, but that doesn't mean everybody else can't."

Susana tenses up at this.

"Leave her alone. What's your problem, anyway?"

"Evan, what's your problem?"

"You. If you really want Gaby, just ask her. Otherwise, shut it."

Everybody turns at this, including Sonia and Hector.

"What?"

"Evan, you don't know what you're saying."

'I know exactly what I'm saying."

"Don't disrespect Sonia like that."

"He's the one disrespecting."

Adrian leaps over Sonia and Gaby to my seat. He lands right on top of me. I try to push him off, but he's too heavy. He lands two, three blows before Hector finally grabs him and throws him off. By this time, security and the police have converged on us. One police officer grabs me by the back of my shirt, and three other police officers grab my legs. They pick me up with a choke hold and carry me back up the aisle. The song abruptly stops and I hear a voice—Chente—over the microphone, scream "Calmen a esos Borrachos!" and I wonder if he is speaking to me. It doesn't seem right that he is. I see another person being carried right behind me, and I assume that it is Adrian. They carry me out to the main level, then through a back door and into a small room. They carry me completely off the floor. I can't even put my legs down for any leverage. It's useless to resist. I don't want to resist. The cop has me in a choke hold, but I can still squeeze out a breath. They carry me down a hall way, then to a door that opens to a room. They throw me in, but not in a violent way. They turn around and shut the door behind them. There is no furniture, so I sit down on the floor. I check my head, but I'm not bleeding anywhere. Adrian did not land any telling blows. I didn't expect this much from him. After I check myself, I sit back down. All of a sudden I am tired, but I don't know why. I sit with my knees up, and I put my head down. So much for that. I look at my watch and it reads three in the morning. I can feel the bass, and it calms me down. The bass vibrates in the whole room. I can feel the vibrations along the walls and in my chest, so I know the concert has started up again. I wonder what Gaby and the rest of them are doing now. I wonder what happened to Adrian. Suddenly the door opens violently, and a cop comes inside. He wants to know what happened. I stick to English. Maybe it will help me.

"I don't know what happened. We were talking, and suddenly he was on top of me."

"They say you started it," the municipal cop informs me.

"I didn't start anything. I certainly didn't leave my seat. Can I go back out?"

The cop looks at me, shrewdly, then exits the room. He's gone for a few minutes, then comes back.

"You are going to stay here until everything is over. Then we might let you go."

"When?"

"We'll wait and see." He shuts the door.

I check my wallet, to see how much money I have left. It might be my only option. Unfortunately, I only have two hundred pesos left. Not nearly enough to pay my way out of trouble. Hopefully, I have help on the outside. I'm sure Hector and Gaby are already making arrangements. I can count on Hector. He should bail me out, if nobody else will. If not, it could be a long night.

* * * *

I know I'm not the only person to be carried out of there. I saw two other fights, in the lower levels, and the cops had to carry those guys out as well. There were multiple doors in the hallway, so that's probably where they are holding everybody. We all have our own room, our own cell. I wonder why they do this. I am a veteran of the drunk-tank, and usually it is a big room with a few benches to house everybody. This is a little different. They house everybody separately. Maybe there is some wisdom in this. If you get into a fight, it's wise to hold people in separate areas. Hopefully, they just treat it like a drunk-tank, and release all of us when everything is over. I'm disappointed that I didn't get any blows in on Adrian. I would have enjoyed reciprocating, but he surprised me. That's the problem with being drunk; it slows down your reaction time. By the time I realized he was on top of me, it was all over. I would have liked to make a better showing, that's all. I owe Adrian a few. I'm also worried about the cops. My situation is precarious. They will probably try to shake money out of me, but that won't work. I don't have any money. They will probably shake money out of Gaby and Hector. If they pay up. Gaby, maybe. Hector, if it comes down to it. He won't let me sit in here. I don't want to go to jail, either. Jail is a risky proposition down in Tijuana. It's always best to avoid that scene. Police brutality holds a different meaning down here than it does in the United States. I've seen the cops do some pretty gruesome things down here. I've only been to jail a few times, on trumped up charges. I've never been jailed in the United States. My jail-time consists of stints in the drunk-tanks of Tijuana and a few other places. Down here in Tijuana, it's always the same. The police will bring you in for almost no good reason at all, just to shake you down. Israel's incident a few years back is a perfect example. He was once accused of accosting a woman on the street, 'grabbing her ass', as the cops put it, and they used that to take us all in to the local tank. It was Israel, Adrian, Eduardo, and myself. It was a long night, and the cops aren't scared to kick a confession out of someone. They will take turns on you until you 'come up' with bail. After a few hours sitting next to drunks pissing on themselves and a transvestite prostitute making out with an old man, they finally released Eduardo to go grab bail money for the rest of us. It probably came out to fifty dollars per person, at which point they released us, with smiles on their faces. Yeah, we just covered their grocery bill for the week. I guess I would be smiling as well. They certainly made their money. That two hundred dollars definitely supplemented their income, but it set us back. We weren't released until five in the morning.

Well, they finally let us out, after I had to watch a seventy year old man make out with a prostitute, right next to a bum who could barely stand up and who had no control of his bodily functions. They put us in that cell on purpose. On the other hand, we were lucky they didn't put us in with anybody worse. That was a long three hours. When you want to sit down, and you can't, it tires a man. I wasn't going to sit down in urine, but I was tired. I was almost tired enough. Then I was worried about Adrian, in the cell with the other criminals. I doubt the three men we were sharing a cell with were criminals; just perverts. Adrian was in with the criminals, and the cops down in Tijuana have their own way of dealing with criminals. They kick them. I couldn't wait to get out, but I doubt the old man cared. Neither did the prostitute. They seemed to be enjoying the cell.

Hopefully, I wasn't in for another night like that. This is just a temporary drunk-tank, and I'm not drunk enough to warrant an overnight stay. I wasn't bad enough that I couldn't walk out of here. I sit down. It feels good to sit down. If you really want to torture somebody, just make them stand up. All day. Don't allow them to sit. That night in the Tijuana jail cell wasn't horrific in itself. What really bothered me was that I couldn't sit down. Here, I can, and I'm left alone.

I could tell by the vibrations that the concert was over. I could no longer feel the bass up against the wall. I could hear footsteps; lots of them. The Arena started to shake with the footsteps. After a half-hour of that, the door opened. I tried to get up, but my leg was asleep. I stumbled as I tried to take a step. The cop looked at me, and I tried to explain that my leg was asleep. I was not that drunk. I could walk on my own. He looked me up and down, then ushered me through the door as I limped. I walked out and saw Hector waiting for me. He was smiling.

"Ok? What's wrong with your leg?"

"I'm fine. My leg just fell asleep. How much do I owe you?"

"We'll talk about that later. I just didn't want them taking you back to the station. They wanted to, but I told them you didn't start it."

"I didn't."

"I know. But you have to be careful. They're looking for drunks who can't control themselves. That's how they make money on a night like this."

"It sucks that they do it."

"Not really. They have families to feed as well."

"Yeah, by shaking down everybody they can."

"That's right," Hector tells me, "just don't make yourself a target. That's all."

"Where is everybody?"

"Out in the parking lot."

"And Adrian?"

"He's next. But he was worse than you. They might not let him out as easily."

"Leave him," I say.

"I can't."

"Do you need help?"

"No, just get out of here. Go outside, get some fresh air. And make sure you don't pass out when you do."

"Ok."

I walked out of the arena, towards our cars. The fresh air did hit me, as Hector said it would. I felt light-headed. That happens when you have been drinking indoors for an extended period of time. When you walk outside, the oxygen hits you, it gives you a buzz. I got dizzy for a moment, and I had to lean up against a car to steady myself. I realized the car was a police-car, and a cop was inside it. He looked at me. I waved at him, then made my way out to the back of the parking lot. Gaby and Sonia were waiting outside the cars, speaking to one another. I always admire their relationship. They are birds of a different feather, but they have the bond of blood. They are as close as anybody I know. Ricardo is passed out, sleeping in Hector's car. He already has his shoes off, and I can see his socks pressed up against the window. I can hear him snoring from here. Eddie is sitting on the ground with his back up against Hector's car. He still has a cup in his hand. He's too drunk to acknowledge me. He sits and mumbles to himself. I look over at Gaby and Sonia. Gaby doesn't speak to me. Sonia does.

"Are you ok.?" Sonia asks me.

"Other than my pride, I'm fine. Is Adrian going to be ok.?"

"Yes, I'm sure Hector will get him out."

Gaby went to the other car, to speak with Israel and Susana. I stayed with Sonia. She was crying now.

"Sonia, I'm sorry."

"No, I'm sorry. I don't know why he gets that way sometimes."

"You don't have to sit there and take it," I tell her.

"I don't. Maybe I won't. Just take it easy, ok? Hopefully he comes out in a few minutes."

"We should probably leave."

"Yes, you probably should."

I walked over to Gaby, who was with Israel and Susana. Susana was crying. So was Gaby. Israel just shrugs at me.

"Gaby, are we ready?"

"Yeah, let's get going."

"What time is it?" I ask Israel.

"Four o'clock."

"I'm hungry," I tell him.

"Yeah, me too."

"Should we grab something to eat?"
"I can eat."
I turn to Gaby. "Do you want to go eat?"
"Yes, whatever."

XIV

We finally arrive at a place called '24', alluding to the fact
that the kitchen in open twenty-four hours a day. The
people of Tijuana just call the place '24'. Our meal is
somber. Fortunately, the police never released Adrian.
They instructed Hector to pick him up at the Otay police
station in a few hours, after they process him. This was a
good move. I didn't want to eat breakfast with Adrian. I
order a large bowl of Menudo. Hector orders the same.
Sonia and Israel order tostadas. I ask Hector how Eddie is
doing, and he replies that he is passed out in the front seat
of his car. Hector is worried that Eddie is going to throw-
up inside his car. I tell him not to worry, I'm sure he will
open the door if it gets that far. Susana keeps pestering
Israel to go. Israel argues that he just ordered food, and he
wants to wait to eat. She grabs the car keys from his pocket, to prevent him from driving. Her parents are waiting for

her. Susana is in tears now, crying at Israel. She really needs to go. I look at my watch, and it's four–thirty in the morning. By the time they cross the border and get home, it will be six in the morning. I wonder, 'what's the point?' If she's in trouble, might as well enjoy it. Susana is not getting home at a respectable hour. After fifteen minutes of crying, Israel finally relents, excuses himself, and walks outside with Susana. He leaves money with Hector. Nobody says goodbye to Suzie. They leave, and the atmosphere amongst our crowd changes a bit. Sonia seems to be enjoying herself, finally. Gaby also seems relaxed. I can smell the food and I am ready for a meal. A meal at four in the morning is more than breakfast. It is not designed to start your day—it is designed to put you to sleep in good standing. I get a sense that I have accomplished something. I feel as if I have gotten away with something. Maybe Adrian landed some blows on me, but I survived, and here I am, eating. He can rot in that cell for all I care.

'24' is just a big open kitchen with a bar surrounding it. The kitchen is large, so the bar can accommodate about fifty people. The kitchen is in the middle of the establishment, and the bar encloses it on all four sides. You can watch the food being prepared. Watching the cooks can whet your appetite. The place is loud and busy. It creates a stark contrast to the early morning. '24' is always crowded, twenty–four hours a day. It is a popular destination in Tijuana. The Menudo is prepared in a huge cauldron. One of the cooks stirs it with an enormous wooden spoon. I know it is going to be good. Gaby seems excited to eat. She finally decides to order a bowl of Menudo, after Hector and I are served our bowls. This is the perfect climate for a bowl of

Menudo. There are about ten different cooks, all running around preparing everything. There are thirty patrons, all spread out around the bar. Most people are young people, like ourselves, finishing up the night. There are a few patrons who appear to be getting ready to go to work. The atmosphere is blended, but it works. If I were going to work, it would be a great scene to start the day. People going to work must be excited by this. Some Tijuanenses are beginning their day, some are ending their day. We enjoy our food, but there's tension in the atmosphere. Adrian is gone. I feel like that is it. Sonia doesn't seem to care. That is the tell-tale sign. The sign I always worry about. Sonia has reached the point where she doesn't care. It doesn't matter whether they get back together or not. The point is: she doesn't care. Adrian is finished. He just doesn't know it yet. I look over at Gaby. She hasn't spoken much since the fight. She hasn't even looked at me. I wonder if I'm finished. My head is starting to throb. The hangover is coming, I can feel it. The bowl of Menudo won't help it, I know this. I mixed too many drinks, and I am going to pay the price in a few hours. You can't go from scotch, to rum, then wine, back to scotch, and finally beer and not pay a heavy toll. My headache sours my mood. Gaby and Sonia are enjoying themselves. So is Hector. They look like they could do it all over again. I couldn't. I excuse myself, go over to the bathroom, and wonder if I am going to throw up. If I do it, might as well be now, but nothing happens. I want to throw up, to feel better, but it doesn't happen. As I stand over the toilet I contemplate whether I should shove my finger down my throat and get it over with, but another guy walks in and that scuttles my idea. I don't return to the table. Gaby, Sonia, and Hector still look good. I walk outside to the parking lot and I still see Ricardo's feet pressed up against the window. Eddie is also there, his head tipped back and sleeping peacefully in the front seat. I don't bother them. I walk onto the street, hail a cab, and head for the border. I don't care if I say goodbye or not. They didn't seem to care, either. I cross the border in an hour, but it seems like a day.

Part III

XV

With the everything coming to a boil, I needed a break. A break from reality, from Gaby, from everybody and everything. I haven't spoken to a soul, other than my coworkers, in over a week. Nobody has called, other than Gaby, and she made it clear that it was urgent. Normally I would jump at that, but not now. I don't bother returning calls; especially that call. I have a suspicion on what that is about, and the less I know the better. Nothing is ever urgent with Gaby, until now. The only human contact I have had is lunch with Rick. He seemed worried, and invited me to eat one afternoon. I took him up on his offer. We had a pleasant lunch in the Gaslamp Quarter, and I explained everything is fine. I've just been feeling a bit run-down, that's all. Other than that, I put my head down. I work, eat, go to sleep, wake up, take care of an errand, go back to work, then back to sleep. That's been my routine since I crossed back. I put in a good hard two week's worth of work, avoid everybody as much as possible, and build up some money for my trip. The less I see of my friends, the easier it is to save money. Bury yourself in work; if you love your job it's not a bad way to storm through life. Everything is much simpler that way. No drama; no games. As usual though, I start getting that wanderlust that lets me know that I am not cut out for a nine-to-five life. September is always a good time of the year to travel further south, so I decided to make my annual pilgrimage to Mulegé. I needed a psychic break from Tijuana and everything it represents.

I take my car to Renteria's, my local mechanic. I always grab a routine tune-up before I make the trip south. Mulegé is my destination, a small oasis town about halfway down the Baja California peninsula, on the Sea of Cortez.

Contemplating a drive down the peninsula is a serious undertaking. Arrangements have to be made. To make the drive through I have to make sure my car is up to the task. There are stretches of highway down there, in the middle of the desert, where you feel you are on Mars. Empty and barren stretches; nothing but desert. You are on your own, and you know it. A few years ago, when I was driving down, I made a game of seeing how long I could drive before a encountered another car passing me by. My record is thirty minutes. A half-hour, and nobody on the road but myself. The only sign of life are the tumbleweeds and the cows grazing on the side of the road. The latter is one of the real hazards of driving in Baja; the cows. Cattle have no sense of danger and no fear of automobiles, until it is too late. Ninety percent of the time, they are content to stay off the side of the road and graze on whatever grass they can find. Once in awhile though, they will decide that the grass is indeed greener on the other side and make a break across the road. Running into a cow or ox at sixty miles per hour is tantamount to slamming into a street pole at the same speed. Cattle on the highway are an extreme road hazard.

Other than that, the trip isn't dangerous; just a bit complicated. Unfortunately, you have to do all of your driving during the day. Somebody once described Baja California at night as the Witching Hour. I can confirm that. I once attempted to start a driving trip from Guerrero Negro to Mulegé at three in the morning to get a head start on things. Bad idea. The highway is pitch-black; street lights don't exist down here. The enormous trucks blow by you at seventy miles an hour and pass within inches of your car. Weird and strange animals that I have never been able to identify run across the road right in front of you. I will never again attempt to drive in Baja California at night. So drive by day, and make sure your tank is always topped off.

After my last shift at work on Friday night, I bid goodbye to Rick, grab a good night's sleep and wake up early to get started. I enjoy waking up early before an extended trip. You wake up excited, full of energy. I woke up this way. It was a good way to start a vacation. I take a long shower and get dressed, packing my things as I prepare myself. I pull out enough cash to last me through the week, pack up my car, and start my drive.

You start in Tijuana, and travel south on Highway 1. It's a toll road all the way down to Ensenada, but that actually works to your advantage. The road is wide and well kept. Once I pass through Tijuana, the drive becomes pleasant. There is nothing pleasant about driving in Tijuana. Driving in Tijuana is a class in stress management, even at night or early in the morning. Roads and highways in Tijuana are virtually unmanageable, and your fellow drivers are extremely aggressive.

Once you clear Tijuana, the road becomes manageable and enjoyable. The lanes are wide, there is a nice shoulder if anything goes wrong, and the view is incredible. Drivers seem to calm down south of Tijuana. Once again, it's the manic energy that permeates everything in that city. South of Tijuana is a completely different story. Many Americans are developing down in this area between Tijuana and Ensenada, and I don't blame them; it's prime real estate. You can see large hotels and condos being constructed with incredible views of the Pacific. The best part of the drive, though, is the approach into Ensenada. I pass an area referred to as 'Salsipuedes,' then make the long curves along a sheltered inlet about five hundred feet above sea level, right along the cliff. I almost forget the road as I am driving, trying to get a better view of the ocean. You can appreciate the Pacific Ocean on a morning like this.

It is two hours to Ensenada from Tijuana, then another two to San Quintín. I pass through wine country, places called Punta Colonet and Santo Tomás, where the L.A. Cetto vineyards are located, then back to the coastline. Once you see the coast line, there are sandy beaches all the way to San Quintín. San Quintín is an ugly little fishing village, but it has a few seafood shacks to turn out the best fried fish or shrimp cocktail anywhere in Baja. San Quintín is always worth a stop, even if it is an eye-sore, just for the food. The mariscos shacks are lined up one after another and shaded by palm groves along the highway. You can't miss them. They are flamboyantly painted to attract attention. San

Quintín is definitely the place to stop for a meal, if nothing else.

I pull into San Quintín around eleven in the morning and drive up to *Mariscos El Paraiso*, one of the mariscos shacks along the highway running through town. I order a small shrimp cocktail and an agua-chile, sit down and drink a couple of beers. I can feel the heat now and the beers go down well. They keep them in a cooler behind the counter. I take my time because I can. Nobody to rush me down here. I am alone and I enjoy it. I speak to the proprietor and he tells me that the clam season is a good one. I agree with him and I order a plate of *almejas ahumadas*. He prepares my plate and serves me two clams, opened up and cooked with olive oil, cheese, and spices. The *alemjas ahumadas* go well with the beer. I scoop out the *pulpo* with a spoon and eat it that way. I squeeze lime in my beer and pour salt into it. This is a good way to drink a beer with prepared clams. It is an excellent meal, and I'm not over-stuffed. I don't want to feel stuffed when I drive, just satis-fied. I sit in the shade with my beer and my plate of *alemjas* and enjoy the fact that I am here with no worries. The proprietor's wife comes over with the bill and asks me where am I staying: am I camping or just down here for the fishing? I reply neither and that I am on my way down to Mulegé. She replies that it is an excellent location but the drive is horrible. The proprietor claims that he lived in Lo-reto, not far south of Mulegé and that it is a nice little town. He tells me that there are a lot of Americans living in Lore-to. I inform him that I am familiar with Loreto but that I prefer Mulegé. He agrees and states that Mulegé has a cer-tain charm. The wife smiles and says that they miss living down there. I agree and say that I wouldn't mind living down there right now. I pay my bill, give my compliments to the proprietor and jump back into my car. The food stands are all along the main highway, so I have no problems navigating the city. There isn't much to look at here anyway, other than a few decent camp-sites along the beach. Once you leave San Quintín, you feel alone.

Next stop is El Rosario, and it is the end of the line in terms of civilization. Baja California Norte ends with El Rosario. And as a village, El Rosario is not impressive. However, it is useful, and convenient. That is the appeal. Other than some very famous lobster burritos, and the last gas station for another seven hours, El Rosario doesn't boast much. It's too quaint for anything, and its working class agricultural roots doesn't make it much of a tourist attraction. Its location makes it ideal for a stop, and it is always a routine rest stop when I travel down the Peninsula.

I drive into town, and pull off right past the gas station. I always stay at the Hotel "El Morro." It's the only decent accommodation in town, and it has a cantina across the street. I pay for my room, grab my bag, drag my cooler inside, take a shower, and I lay down and just stare at the ceiling for an hour. The air conditioning is turned up, as it has to be in Baja. It's about ninety degrees outside. The drone of the antiquated air conditioning helps me meditate. It's one of those old wall units, and it's loud, but it does the job. After everything that has happened this summer, it's nice to lay here, in an air conditioned hotel room, by myself, and not be bothered. I didn't tell anybody I was coming down, other than Gaby and my family. She didn't need to be told though, she could have guessed easy enough. She knows me by now, knows that I'm down here. She never asks to come, though. Baja "isn't her scene"; her words exactly. I lay there, staring at the ceiling, listening to the air conditioning, and my mind keeps running. Gaby, Adrian and Sonia, Ricardo, Israel and Susana. It feels good to just stare at a ceiling with the air conditioning on, out of tune with reality. Once in awhile, a man needs to isolate himself from reality. Nobody bothers me here in the Hotel. Nobody knows I'm here. It's a bit dangerous to travel down here without anyone knowing my destination, but I don't care. It's worth it. Cell phones don't work down here, for the most part, and I like it that way. I hope Baja never figures that one out. I don't want any cell phones to work down here. They should outlaw it. Never put up those damned cell phone towers here. Baja doesn't need them. I reach over to my cooler and pull out a beer. Tecate makes a good light beer. Perfect for this climate. A light Pilsner or Lager is what you need in Baja. No IPA's, Stouts, or anything of the like. Those types of beer are too heavy for this climate. Drinking a few Guinness' and then stepping out to ninety degree heat can bring about a failure in health. You need something refreshing. You have to drink according to climate, to temperament. Today, it's light beer.

My mind continues to work through everything. Gaby? She was acting weird, in the end. She wouldn't drink much that last night at the Palenque. That fact bothers me. Why wouldn't she drink? My imagination races, because there are only so many reasons why a woman declines to drink. I guess I'm going to have to find a real job. Adrian and Sonia splitting up? Well, that was coming. I saw it coming a mile away. Israel and Susana? Good luck with her. Israel's parent's are going to struggle with that. It can't be healthy that I am surrounded by dysfunctional relationships, mine being the most erratic. But whatever. Down here, the problem doesn't seem that bad. I'm more confident down here. Problems don't feel like problems down here. I don't even feel like music right now. I need quiet. I'm not even tired. I lay on my back on top of the bed listening to the hum of the air conditioner and I occupy myself by counting the holes in the ceiling tiles.

* * * *

Once my meditation is over, I cross the street for a beer or two. The cantina "El Morro" is a straight dive bar, locals only; and these are working class locals. Agricultural laborers looking to cool off with a cahuama of Tecate. The bartender recognizes me.

"¿Que paso, Güero?"

"Nada. Voy para Mulegé. Necesito un descanso."

He laughs. '¿Descanso? ¿De que?"

"Todo."

He wags his finger at me. "Gabachos y sus problemas. No tiene problemas. No tiene nada."

I agree with him. What problems do I have? He laughs again, and reaches for a Cahuama. It is cold. All the beer here in the Cantina 'El Morro' is cold. He then grabs a frosty mug out of the refridgerator and hands it to me.

"Para sus problemas." We both laugh. That's a good bartender.

The beer is cold, as it should be. I pour it in the mug. Flakes of ice from the bottom of the mug break off and float at the top of my beer. Everything is cold here. When you live in perpetual ninety degree heat, an ice cold beer is a priority. Not like the warm beers you'll get served in San Diego. Here, they appreciate the cold. It's important. They will spend the extra hundred pesos a month in electricity to keep the beer cold. The refrigerator itself is old, and that is the key. It is something I have noticed. The new refrigerators are all designed to be more efficient, work quietly, and consume as little energy as possible. I respect that. The refrigerator in the cantina 'El Morro' though is a different breed of animal compared to the ultra efficient models of the North. This fridge looks to be about forty years old; an industrial strength giant. It's huge, and it's loud. It must weigh half-a-ton. But you know the beer coming out of it is going to border freezing. That's the way it should be. Always look for a bar with an ancient industrial strength refrigerator. I drink my industrial-strength cold beer, give my regards to the bartender, then cross the street. I linger as I watch an old man on a bicycle carrying two small palm trees. The trees are strapped to either side of his bike, and they stand about eight feet high. The balancing act looks ridiculous, but he pulls it off. I worry about him. He is riding on the side of the road, with cars passing by, and his bike is swerving from side to side, trying to balance the palm trees. One slip and he could easily crash into one of the passing cars, but he doesn't. He seems to have it figured out. As I watch him, I think to myself: If that old man can figure out how to balance two eight-foot palm trees strapped to the back of his bike, I can figure out my balancing act with Gaby. I watch him disappear down the road, into the sunset, then I walk back to my room to crash for the night. It's a long drive to Mulegé tomorrow.

XVI

The road south of El Rosario turns into an adventure. Here, you enter the real desert. It's a small drive out of the valley where El Rosario sits, then up to the high desert where the rest of the trip is made. The high desert here takes a turn for the macabre. The Cirio trees are the defining characteristic of the landscape, and they define Baja. They are ugly and beautiful at the same time. At first glance, you swear they are the ugliest trees you have ever seen. They appear to be large cacti, overgrown and with ugly warts and hair. They look like organic scarecrows. But on closer inspection, you begin to appreciate a tree, or any other living organism that can thrive and reproduce in this climate. As I drive south, the Cirio trees and the enormous rocks dominate the landscape.

There is only one pit stop between El Rosario and Guerrero Negro, and that is a dusty place called Cataviña. It's smack in the middle of the desert, and it only has one shop in town, a dirty little *abarrotes* where you can grab some ice and a few snacks. It has a dried up gas station that was abandoned about ten years ago. I pull right off the highway, and park in front of the store. Everything in Cataviña is right off the highway. I walk up to the abarrotes and automatically get approached by the resident bum of Cataviña. His gig is always the same; he's an ex-pat 'passing through' on his way back to the States after twenty years on the lamb down in Baja. He always needs a little cash or some spare change to make it back up to the States for his "surgery." He has needed that surgery for twenty years.

"Hey, brother," he asks me, "any pesos? I'm trying to get back up to San Diego and I'm stuck here."

"C'mon, I think you've been stuck here for years."

He laughs.

"I have. I just need a drink right now. It's hot."

I laugh, "Fuck, of course it's hot. It must be a hundred degrees out here." I stare at him for a second or two. "How long have you been here?"

"Oh, in and out."

"Alright, here you go."

I've been giving this guy change for the past few years, every time I pass by on my way down to Baja. His situation never changes, and he is never going to make it back up to Tijuana or San Diego for his surgery. He is Cataviña's resident bum. He wears his fishing shirt from La Paz; the one they sell to tourists. The shirt has a map of Baja California on it, and it lists all the different types of fish you can catch in Baja. It's also has ten years of dirt on it, although it does look like he washes it about once a month. He wears jeans that were cut off to make shorts. He has a pair of broken down sandals on his crusty feet. His skin is so leathery he doesn't bother with sunscreen anymore. I figure he was once on his way back up to the States, and never figured a way out. He's been here for years, and this is his home. His gig is simple; pick up money from tourists and people passing through. Everybody stops in Cataviña, because they have to. It's the only game in town in the middle of the desert. It is hours either way to civilization. I doubt he has to make much to survive here.

"You have a smoke?" he asks me.

"Yes." I pass him my pack. I can see the waves of heat rolling off the asphalt of the road. Damn, it's hot. Smoking a cigarette in one-hundred degree heat is a special skill. I respect it.

"You need anything else?"

"Twenty pesos or a couple bucks would be great."

"I'll give you five dollars if you really tell me how long you've been here."

He laughs, and shows his gnarled teeth. Definitely a tweaker. You can tell by the teeth. When you hit that stuff long enough, the teeth are always the first to go.

"Years, brother. Years. I stopped counting."

"Why?"

"I'm alright here. I head down to Guerrero Negro from time to time. If I want to work, maybe up to El Rosario. But I haven't been up to El Rosario in ages."

"So, Cataviña is the place to be, huh?"

"It is for me. Once you get used to the heat, everything is fine. I help with the shop a little bit, and if anybody needs help I do what I can."

"There you go."

His teeth might be a sign as to how he has made a living down here. He could be a small time smack dealer, especially to drivers who need that extra rush to get wherever they need to get. The good truck drivers make their haul at night down here, and a quick pit stop in Cataviña in the dead of night for a dose of smack will do the trick and take care of any weariness for a driver with a non-stop haul to La Paz or Los Cabos. There's money to be made in a venture like that.

And that is the Cataviña bum. He checked out of society years ago, and he doesn't seem that far gone to me, anyway. Some men just reach the point where they are ready to check out. Cataviña is as good a place as any. If he is trying to avoid attention, it's the perfect spot.

I pull out of Cataviña, but no worries, I'll be back in a week. I doubt the bum will even remember me; he never does. It's the same gig, all over again in another week.

Four hours on the road, with nothing to look at except cattle and Cirio trees, and I finally pass the crossroads to Bahía de Los Angeles. The Americans that pass down this way refer to it as 'L.A.' Bay, and it has a few outdoor activities to choose from. 'L.A.' Bay is about another hour from the highway. I continue south and I finally reach Guerrero Negro. It's right on the border of Baja California Norte and Baja California Sur. Guerrero Negro is the midway point, about twelve hours straight from Tijuana. Guerrero Negro is small and dusty; a one street town. The only advantages to G.N. are the decent accommodations and the Pemex gas station. Filling the tank is a necessity in Guerrero Negro. That's the one challenge in Baja. Up in the States, gas stations are abundant. You never have to worry about running out of gas. Baja is a different story. You have to plan your trip around gas stations. Emptying your tank is a reality down here, and getting stranded out here can be life threatening. That's why I always stop in El Rosario before I head south to G.N.

I cross the agricultural inspection, because I'm crossing a state line. They spray my car with a pesticide, while I'm still in it, charge me twenty pesos, then I continue my journey to Mulegé. I check my watch, and it's already noon. I will try to make it all the way to Mulegé, but I can stay in Santa Rosalía if it comes down to it. Santa Rosalía is the first stop on the Sea of Cortez. Mulegé is further south, another hour or so. Santa Rosalía is the first real 'Baja' stop, and it is bizarre, to say the least. It used to be an old French mining town, back in the 19th century. The old mining complex and industrial equipment is still there. There is also a hotel, designed by Gustav Eiffel himself. The entire hotel was imported part by part from France back in the 19th century and reconstructed in Santa Rosalía. It still exists, and serves guests. It is always a good place to stay, and the accommodations are unique. It is also typical Baja weirdness. What is a hotel designed by Gustav Eiffel doing in Santa Rosalía? Nobody knows, but there it is, and I recommend it.

I finally make it in to Mulegé about an hour before sunset, and I immediately drive south to Bahía Concepción, where all the beaches and bungalows are. My place is Playa Naranjos, where they rent *palapas* with running water. The *palapa* is the best option down in Mulegé. Palapas are small shacks, made of wood, and they have screened windows all around. Some even come with a small kitchenette. For fifteen dollars a night, you can't beat it. The person that runs Playa Naranjos is a middle-aged lady who owns the restaurant right in the center of the community. She smiles when she sees me.

"¿Hola, Señora, cómo esta?" I ask her. "Buen clima, eh?"

"Claro, claro, pero este dia solamente. Ayer hubo una tormenta, pero no mas."

"¿Hay lluvia, aquí en Septiembre?"

"Si, ayer. Mucho, pero cielos despejados ahora y mañana."

"¿Y mi Palapa?"

"Oy, listo para ti. ¿Quiere electricidad, no?"

"Claro que sí."

"Precio con electricidad...dos cientos pesos. ¿Cuantas noches?"

"Probablemente cuatro."

"Ok Güero, vamos."

We walk over to the palapa, which was right up on the shoreline, along with a string of other palapas, and a few R.V.'s with boats.

"¿Cuantos personas hay aquí?"

"Ahorita, solamente tres palapas. Dos R.V.'s tambien. En dos o tres semanas, llega mas gente."

She opens the door for me, glances in the room, and gives me the keys. I walk in and immediately started opening all of the windows. In a palapa like this, the wall is almost entirely windows. It allows the breeze to cool down the entire place. Also, the back door opens directly to the beach. I stop in, throw my bags down, put on my swim trunks, and walk right into the water. I swim out about a hundred yards or so, where the water is chest deep. The water is warm, as it should be. The water is not salty, as it is on the Pacific side. Swimming in the Sea of Cortez is a cross between a lake and a swimming pool. You get all of the advantages of swimming in a lake and all of the advantages of swimming in a sea, with none of the disadvantages. There is no current to fight in the Bahía, the water is warm, it's full of fish, and the water visibility can stretch a mile or two. This is why I come down here. I see shadows playing out all over the water, so I know I don't have much more time before I have to head in. The sun is about to set, but I can get in a good twenty minutes before I have to swim in for the night. I love swimming when the sun is setting, however here in Mulegé the sun sets over the mountains, not over the water. This is always the best time to do things in the Baja desert; in the evening. It is when the air is coolest. I back-float in the water, and I hear small fish jumping all over the place. You can hear them all night. The fish jump out of the water, waiting to be caught. After a few minutes of listening to the fish, I swim back in and dry off.

There are no electricity lines in Playa Naranjos. It is actually a small community of palapas about ten minutes off the main road. At about eight o'clock at night, a generator kicks in, giving electricity to the entire community. The generator runs from eight in the evening to about four in the morning, depending on how much gasoline the owner puts in the night before. There is about an hour of darkness though, between seven and eight o'clock. Unless you bring your own lights sources, you have to suck up the hour in darkness. I walk over to the restaurant in the middle of the community, the one the proprietress owns, where they have their own separate generator, and wait it out. When the main generator kicks in you can hear it, and the whole community comes alive again. I walk back across to my palapa. The drive down here has finally caught up with me. The palapa is comfortable enough, once you open up all the windows. The breeze flows right through. With the breeze, and my bed right underneath the window, it turns into a comfortable night.

XVII

I wake up about eight in the morning, and walk out the back door onto the porch, then right into the water. In Playa Naranjos, you don't need a shower. All you need is the Bahía Concepción to wake you up. The Bahía Concepción is a protected bay in the Sea of Cortez. That makes it perfect for swimming, snorkeling, fishing, and just about every water activity you can think of, other than surfing. Jacques Cousteau once referred to the Sea of Cortez as the Aquarium of the Ocean, and his analogy is correct. It's time to enjoy the largest aquarium in the world. I slept in my swim trunks, so I don't have to change. I just get up from my hammock, stretch out a bit so I don't cramp up, and walk out into the water. There's nothing better than to swim in the morning, and to wake up and be able to swim right outside your back door. I can do this in Playa Naranjos. A good swim in the morning can give you energy all day long. If you can, always do some sort of physical exercise in the morning, before your day. It actually helps rather than hinders the rest of your day. I always feel lethargic in the afternoon if I didn't get any activity in the morning. Playa Naranjos has a small sand beach, but is covered by rocks underneath the water. The water is perfect, and I swim for thirty minutes. A flock of birds, looking like pelicans, fly out from the Bahía towards the open water. They fly in a single file line, one after another, about twelve in total. Even their wings are in synch, and I wonder how they do that. They fly so close together, in a line, that their noses touch the other's backside. Maybe it helps with the aerodynamics to fly that way. They fly in straight line, about three feet off the surface of the water. I get the impression they are going to work for the day. I feel lazy, because those birds are going off to work this morning and I am just lying here, treading water and enjoying the sunrise.

After my morning swim in Playa Naranjos, I clean myself up, eat a sandwich I had packed, and drive back up to Mulegé. Mulegé is a small town located along a river. It is an Oasis in the desert. It is small, but nice, especially at this time of the year. The people are always friendly. The streets are small and narrow, and I stop by a store on the corner of one of the town squares. Mulegé has a European feel, with the narrow streets and small town-squares to navigate around. I park my car along one of the squares and walk into a grocery store. I stock up on ice, beer, and some food. I have a conversation with one of the employees there. I am the only customer in the store at this time in the morning. She is nice, agreeable, and tells me the town is just barely getting back on their feet after the small Hurricane that struck last fall. I tell her I was down here last fall, but before the Hurricane struck. She tells me I was lucky, because it was horrible. No electricity, no running water, nothing. I tell her that wouldn't bother me. She replies that it bothered her. She asks me where I am going. I tell her that I am going back down to the Bahía. She recommends that I visit Playa El Burro, or Playa Requesón. I agree, and tell her that indeed Playa Requesón is my destination. I inform her that if she is interested she can join me down there anytime today. I will be down there all day. She tells me thanks, but no thanks. I grab my bags and wave goodbye. When I get to my car, I stock the beer and the bottled water in my cooler, then place the ingredients for sandwiches in another bag. I make sure there is plenty of ice in the cooler, because that is important. I double-check that I have everything I need: snorkeling gear, food, change of clothes, chair, cooler, sun-screen, first-aid kit. Then I drive out of the town square and back onto the highway.

I head back down to a beach called Playa Requesón. Requesón is further south on the Bahía, and you have to take a small road off the main highway to get there. The road is in bad repair, and my car barely makes it. I drive a small Japanese car, which isn't best suited for Baja-type terrain. After maneuvering around some rocks and avoiding a few craters that pass for pot-holes, I make it. It is by far the best beach in Baja, and virtually untouched. The sand is white, and fine. Playa Requesón refers to a very small island just off the beach, Requesón Island. The island is only a few hundred yards from the beach, and only a quarter-mile in diameter. If the tide is low, a spit of sand connects the beach to the island, and you can walk across the spit to the island. If the tide is high, you can still walk across, about waist deep in water. The water is crystal clear, and the snorkeling is beautiful. The sand is so white, it hurts my eyes in the midday sun. I grab my beach Palapa, make sure there is enough shade, set up my chair and my cooler, crack open a beer, and enjoy a beautiful beach all to myself.

After a couple beers, I walk out to the sand bridge to Isla Requesón. I have my snorkel gear, and there is a good snorkeling spot right off the island. The tide is high right now, so I have to wade the sand bridge. The deepest I reach is my thighs, but the sand is soft under my feet, so the going is slow. It is also refreshing. Once I reach my spot, I put on my fins, always a tricky movement in the sand, put on my goggles and snorkel, and swim out to the island. The white sand underneath gives the water a pool-water quality. The fish, bright and clear with the sand as a backdrop, glitter in the sun. Parrot fish, yellowtail, angelfish, eels, and everything you need is right there. There is no current, so no current to fight as I snorkel along. The fish aren't aggressive, or afraid of me. They seem to imbibe the qualities of the Peninsula, live and let live. There is a different quality and pace to life down here, and it is the antithesis of life in the North. The fish seem to understand this. They know I'm not out to catch them, just observe them. I make up my mind to snorkel to the other side of the island, to deeper water, to see if I can spot anything unusual. It's a long swim, but you don't get as tired when you snorkel, as opposed to swimming. Snorkeling is a more streamlined activity than swimming; you use fewer muscles, and therefore less effort. I can snorkel for hours, but I can only swim for twenty to thirty minutes. I cruise around to the other side of the island. This takes me about ten minutes of constant snorkeling, but it does not tire me. Once I reach the other side of the island, I'm exposed to the deeper waters of the Bahía, and I can feel the current now. The Snorkeling gets difficult, and intense. I dive down to the bottom a few times, looking under a few rocks. The water is clear, and easy to navigate. There is no swell because of the Bahía. I can feel the current and I fight the current, and that is always a bad proposition. You can never fight an ocean current and win. Since I'm alone, I turn around and make my way back. No reason to get tired and in trouble out here. A cramp now can have consequences. Nobody knows I'm here. I make my way back around the island, spot a Moray Eel between two rocks, count myself lucky, and resurface back on the beach of the Island. I'm tired, but it is a good feeling. There's being tired and feeling bad, and then there is being tired and feeling good. This was the good feeling. Even though your body is tired, it feels right. I always get this sensation after I swim. I walk around back to the sand bridge, clean my snorkel in the water, and sit down for a few minutes in the sun. I crave a beer, so I head back up to my palapa and open my cooler. Another car has pulled up to the beach, and a guy comes out and opens his trunk, pulling out a few boxes. He is selling hats, trinkets, and whatever else you need.

"Amigo, ¿Comó esta? Habla Español?"

I lie. "No, Inglés."

"But your Spanish is good."

"How do you know?"

"I can tell."

"Your English is also good."

He nods. "You need anything?"

"A good hat, to protect from the sun." Some hats are purely decorative, designed to make you look good. I needed a hat to do a job; protect me from the sun.

"I have plenty of hats."

"Claro que sí."

I choose a hat, then pay. We both wipe our brow. It is getting hot. He appears to be friendly, so I ask him.

"¿Quieres sombra? ¿Necesita tomar?"

"Sí, y sí."

We walk over to the palapa, and I open the cooler for him. He grabs a Tecate.

"¿Dónde está la gente?" I ask him. "Where are the Canadians?"

"Oh, the Canadians get down here. Two, three weeks or so. They bring their R.V.s and they park them right on the beach."

"They shouldn't be allowed to do that."

"They do. And they have money, so nobody bothers."

"Still, they shouldn't park on the beach like that. It's disrespectful."

"I agree, but they bring money."

"Do they bring beer?" I ask. We both laugh.

"Yes. The Canadians like to drink beer."

"They just shouldn't park on the beach, that's all."

"I agree. But they have nothing like this in Canada. They like it here."

"Sure, it beats a freezing winter, which is what they deal with every year. And your English is good."

"It has to be."

"True."

The wind whistles along the water, and I can hear every detail.

"Do you have family?"

"Yes. Two daughters."

"Here, in Mulegé?"

"Yes. We live here."

"Not a bad place to live. Another beer?"

"Yes, please."

I grab two more beers from my cooler.

"I could live down here," I inform him.

"Only certain people can. My older daughter already wants to leave. It's tough for young people."

"Not enough to do?"

"They don't see the value down here. Not yet."

"I see the value."

"I agree."

We drink the rest in silence. It is so quiet, you can hear the wind and nothing else.

* * * *

Mulegé has a small airport, but it doesn't service most major airlines. Not enough tourists know about the place, and the runway is too short to handle a larger airplane. However, you can find a flight about once a week from Ensenada on a small charter airplane, the propeller type. They usually land on Wednesdays. This Wednesday, Gaby is going to be on that flight. She got word to me through email. Not my email, but the email of the proprietress that runs Playa Naranjos. Yesterday morning a young man, one of the employees of the community, came walking to my palapa with a printout of an email he received. Gaby knows I always stay in Playa Naranjos. The message was simple and it was dated yesterday:

Evan-
I'm flying down from Ensenada tomorrow. Can you pick me up at the airport? They told me the plane will be flying straight in. Please call me if you can, or leave a message with my parents.
-Gaby

'Well', I think to myself, that means Mulegé all fucked up. I wanted to commission a boat to take me out trolling for yellow-tail, but that's not going to happen now.

I am shocked she would come down without confirming first that I was in Mulegé. I might have stopped in San Ignacio, or gone further south to Loreto. Who knows? I know the conversation she wants to have, and I'm not in the mood for it. And now she's invading my space, my world down here. I don't deal with drama down here; that's why I come. To avoid all that trouble. Now, trouble is coming down my way. Well, I guess it was bound to happen. You can't always run away from your problems, and this was a problem. She wants to talk it out, right now, and I don't. I am surprised to see the email. She has never expressed much interest in going to the beach, any beach, even though she lives in Tijuana and San Diego.

Then it occurs to me. I'm going to have to leave Playa Naranjos. No way is Gaby going to stay here. No hot water, no air conditioning, no amenities. Alternatives started to run through my mind. Playa El Burro is beautiful, with palapas, but nothing in Gaby's comfort zone. Playa Santispac was arguably the beach in Mulegé, but the accommodations are worse than Naranjos. We will probably have to stay in Playa Buenaventura, which has a motel right on the beach. It's an odd looking building, single story, made of stone, but the accommodations are decent, with AC and a bar with a small restaurant. It just frustrates me that I have to uproot myself here from Playa Naranjos, where I was just settling in, and move over to Buenaventura. It has to be. Gaby is particular, and she will refuse to stay in Naranjos. So I walk over to the restaurant and explain my situation to the landlady. She is sad to see me leave so soon, but I explain that my plans have changed. I tell her that I don't want to leave either, but I have no choice. I pay my rent and pack up my car. Playa Buenaventura is about twenty minutes down from Naranjos, on the southern end of Bahía Concepción. I drive down, and inquire.

"¿Tiene cuartos?'

"¿Cuántos?"

"Uno. Matrimonio."

He checks his ledger, making a big show out of it. It's a ridiculous endeavor. I know he knows what is available.

"Sí. ¿Cuantas noches?"

"Dos."

He nods, then takes my credit card. I check out the room, it looks fine, put my luggage in, and then drive back up to Mulegé. Gaby's plane should be arriving in about two hours. That's the thing about Gaby. I try to avoid problems. She seeks them out. I'll duck down to Baja to get away from it. She will come down to Baja looking for it. Well, here we go.

Her plane arrived late, but they finally landed. I walk right up to the loading dock; that's how lax security is in a small airport. You have to grab your own luggage out of the plane. Gaby seemed fine. Herself, anyway. We greet each other and she hugs me.

"So, this is the great Mulegé. It's weird. I expected a dusty desert town. There are trees everywhere."

"I told you."

I take hold of her luggage and we walk back to my car. I open the door for her and pack her suitcase in the trunk. We start our drive back down to the beaches.

"Why are there so many trees here?" she asks. "I thought it was all desert in Baja."

"Mulegé is an oasis. There's plenty of water here."

"Are those palm trees? There are thousands of them!"

"Some are palm trees. Most are date trees."

"Oh, is that why they have that yellow stuff on them?"

"Yes. They just finished the harvest. Between here and San Ignacio, they do well. They can make just about any dish using dates."

She stares at the trees, then turns to me.

"Where are we staying?"

"A hotel on the beach, a little further south."

"Is it nice?"

"Nice enough."

"Does it have a restaurant?"

"Yes, it has a restaurant," I reassure her, "and a bar."

She seemed to relax after that. The telltale sign of a decent Hotel is the presence of a bar. The more elegant the bar, and adjoining restaurant, the better the accommodations. The Buenaventura has a bar overlooking the beach. You can rent Kayaks outside. You can eat very well inside. It's a nice place. I convey this to Gaby.

"It's fine. I don't need anything special."

We finally pull up to Playa Buenaventura and I show Gaby the room.

"I'm tired. Can we lay down for a minute? I can use a nap."

"Sure."

We lie down together, and silence ensues. We don't need to communicate verbally. Everything has already been said. Gaby closes her eyes, but I can hear her breathing and I know she is still awake. I don't say anything. After about twenty minutes, I hear her breathing change and I know she is asleep. I can't sleep, so I get up, go outside to the bar and order a beer. I watch the shadows creep over the hills, and slowly fold over the Bahía Concepción. The beaches here face east, so you can only view the sunrise. The sunset disappears over the mountains behind me. I see a flock of birds heading back in after their day out over the ocean. I wonder what they do all day, together like that. I swear it's the same flight of birds I saw leave together the other day out of Playa Naranjos, but I could be wrong. It grows dark when Gaby wakes up and finally meets me at the bar. The lights start to turn on.

"So, what are we doing tomorrow?"

I turn around and smile.

"Something? Who says we are doing something? Let me tell you a little something about this place. Down in Baja, you do nothing. Even when you do something, you call it 'nothing.'"

"Ok, ok. So... when are going to do nothing?"

"Well, we can go swimming tomorrow morning. That's nothing. We can rent a kayak. That's nothing. We can rent some tanks and go Diving."

"Wait, Scuba Diving? I can count that as something."

"You're right. Snorkeling, then. Let's go snorkeling. That's nothing."

"How about fishing? Don't you like to fish?"

"Do you want to go out on a boat?" I ask.

"No, not in my condition. I'm queasy as it is. Anyway, fishing might be defined as something. I'm not interested in fishing."

"No, it's only something if you cook and then eat the fish you catch. Just going out on a boat and pulling them is nothing."

"I can still swim?"

"Sure."

"How about a drink?"

We both laugh.

It stays silent for awhile. The hotel appears to be empty. It's just us and another couple in the restaurant. They ignore us, we ignore them. The silence is instructive. It tells me everything I need to know about Gaby and myself. If you can sit in comfortable silence with somebody else, and no awkwardness, then you can do anything together. The silence, and the sunset behind us, shares in our complicity.

"I don't know how you are going to handle it; it's a long time without alcohol."

"I'm fine. I can't imagine you doing it though."

"True, true."

Gaby and I stare at the last rays of sunshine on the Bahía. The shadows begin to creep over the water. The Bahía flickers between light and shadow.

"Wouldn't it be nice to just stay down here, and not go back," she says.

"I'm surprised to hear you say that," I tell her. "Believe me, it's not the first time that has crossed my mind."

"Yes, it's pleasant to think it, anyway."

This work of fiction is dedicated to my wife and daughter, who have to deal with my strange idiosyncrasies, and my family, because without their support this book would not have been possible.

Also, to my *other* family who reside and enjoy life on either side of the border. Much of the material in this book was inspired by them. When I joined that crazy family over ten years ago, they welcomed this strange Gringo with open arms, as is their custom. Gracias. Mahalo.

—T.A. Pickett

Trixia,

hope you enjoy
the book! Thanks
for the support.

— Tucker Pickett